NOAH'S REVELATION
RED LODGE BEARS - BOOK TWO

KAYLA GABRIEL

Noah's Revelation: Copyright © 2019 by Kayla Gabriel

All Rights Reserved. No part of this book may be reproduced or transmitted in any form or by any means, electrical, digital or mechanical including but not limited to photocopying, recording, scanning or by any type of data storage and retrieval system without express, written permission from the author.

Published by Kayla Gabriel
Gabriel, Kayla
Noah's Revelation

Cover design copyright 2019 by Kayla Gabriel, Author

Images/Photo Credit: Deposit Photos: photocosma, kiuikson

This book has been previously published.

GET A FREE BOOK!

Join my mailing list to be the first to know of new releases, free books, special prices and other author giveaways.

http://freeshifterromance.com

ONE

"Well, what do you think?" Aubrey asked. She paused on the steps leading down into the living room from the kitchen, an expectant expression on her face. From his spot on the couch, the bright kitchen light showcased Aubrey's hourglass silhouette to perfection.

"About you?" Luke asked, letting his gaze travel over her from head to foot. Long, dark red locks flowed down her back and shoulders, forming thick waves that ended at her waist. She wore a form-fitting black work dress with a thin patent-leather belt adorning her waist. Coupled with her signature cherry-red stiletto heels, the ensemble made the most of every delicious inch of her curvy frame.

Luke gave her a slow, wicked smile, and Aubrey gave a huff of pretend exasperation.

"Not of me, of the house!" she said, rolling her eyes. She stepped down, her heels clicking neatly on the floor, the swish of her hips distracting him… again.

Settling herself on the couch next to Luke, Aubrey picked up the laptop that he'd discarded on the coffee table. She worked for a moment, brow furrowing, until she turned the laptop back to him.

"This is the one I like the most, I think," Aubrey said. "The house is bigger than what I had planned to get just for myself, but there's a nice yard. And… it's near a lot of good schools."

"Schools, huh?" Luke asked, arching a dark brow. "Didn't know we were worried about that just yet."

Aubrey flushed to the fiery roots of her hair, lifting a shoulder in a casual shrug.

"Just looking out for our interests, that's all," she said.

Luke leaned over and dropped a kiss on her bare shoulder before turning his attention back to the laptop. His fingers flicked over the track pad as he perused the photos Aubrey had presented, pursing his lips thoughtfully. It really was a beautiful house, big and bright and airy.

He closed the laptop with a snap, giving Aubrey a long look.

"Here's the thing about houses—" he started, but his mate cut him off.

"Is it too much? It's too big, isn't it? Do you think we're rushing things, getting a house when we haven't even had the wedding yet?" Aubrey gushed, twining her fingers in her lap.

"Aub," Luke sighed.

"It's okay, we can just wait," Aubrey said.

The way her shoulders sagged at the thought nearly made him chuckle. When his mate felt something, she felt it with her whole heart, invested her all her considerable force into it. Luke reached out and clasped her hand, running his thumb over the glittering diamond and sapphire ring adorning her left hand. The ring he'd put on her finger when he'd asked her to be his mate, just after promising that he'd give her the entire world.

He'd meant every word, and nothing would diminish his commitment to Aubrey Rose Umbridge. If anything, his obsession with her, with seeing her happy and sated, grew with each passing day they spent together.

"Aubrey," Luke said, cutting her off before she could continue her diatribe. "The thing about houses is that it is completely up to you. San Francisco is your city, you know it best. And I don't care how many bedrooms there are, or what the yard looks like, or whether we have walk-in closets. That's all just icing on the cake, honey."

Aubrey's instant and obvious relief made him chuckle.

"Are you sure, Luke?" she asked, turning her hand to lace her fingers with his.

"I'm very sure. You like the house, let's get the house and fill it with all our furniture and clothes… and maybe some kids for those great schools, huh?"

Aubrey blushed again, but her lips twitched into a soft smile.

"I like the sound of that," she whispered, cupping his jaw and brushing her lips against his.

Luke's phone vibrated, making them both jump. He sighed when he saw the text from his brother Gavin.

Finn and Noah still haven't hashed it out. Can't even get them into a room together, read the text. Another buzz, another text. This one read: *Could really use the oldest brother's help here…*

Luke looked up at Aubrey, an odd smile lifting the corners of his lips.

"How do you feel about a quick trip to Montana?" he asked.

TWO

*L*uke stood on the Lodge's wraparound porch, staring out into the darkness. It felt so strange, being back here. So quiet and peaceful. His mate's laughter drifted out from the living room, where Luke's mother was no doubt entertaining Aubrey with a deluge of embarrassing childhood photos of Luke and his brothers. Though he'd never doubted Aubrey's worth, the fact that she and his mother had taken to each other immediately had eased something deep inside Luke's consciousness.

For all his mate's generosity and strength and beauty, she could be harsh at times. Not, Luke reflected, entirely unlike Genny Beran herself. Wisdom said that men married their mothers, after all. When he'd watched Aubrey and his mother together, he could understand that sentiment. They were both opinionated but supportive, sweet but fierce, giving and demanding.

Luke tensed at the sound of bare feet behind him. He forced himself to stay still, reminding himself that this place was safe. In another moment, he turned to find Noah just behind him.

"Run?" Luke asked his brother.

Noah arched a brow, probably surprised because Luke usually preferred solitude in all things. Noah shrugged and nodded, and they both stepped down from the porch. The familiar snaps and rends and creaks sounded softly in the night as they both shifted, leaving two massive Grizzlies standing side by side.

Luke took off at a lope, heading for a favorite spot less than a mile away. Noah ambled along at his side; even in their bear forms, Luke could tell that something was bothering him. The tension with Finn seemed to be wearing him down.

Luke took the long way, circling around to a stone outcropping that the Beran boys had favored as children. Just below was a small pond, a place that they visited often in the summer months. Now, though, Luke intended to talk to Noah, try to fix things between him and Finn. Knowing the twins for every moment of their lives, Luke had no question of whether Noah was somehow the cause of the fight. It simply wasn't in Finn to instigate trouble with his brother.

Luke shifted and stretched, shaking off the after-effects of the change. He sprawled out on one side of of broad, flat rock, lying on his back and staring up at the stars. Noah found a spot several feet away, lying back and tucking his hands behind his head as he watched the star-laden skies.

For a long time, neither of them spoke. Luke was content to watch and listen, soaking in all the natural beauty that he missed so desperately every time he stepped foot in the city, any city. He sensed Noah's breathing evening out, and knew he had to speak up if he was going to talk to his brother before Noah drifted off.

"Did you know Pa has a twin brother?" Luke asked. He didn't look over at Noah, but he could tell that his brother was no longer drowsing.

"No," Noah said after a long moment of silence, his voice tense. Somehow he could tell what Luke wanted to talk about, and he was already being bullheaded about it.

"Hear me out. I don't ask you a lot of favors," Luke insisted. When Noah remained still and quiet, he continued. "Pa had a twin, a few minutes older than him. Jericho."

Several long beats passed.

"Had?" Noah asked, his curiosity getting the better of him.

"Had. I only know bits and pieces of the story, but Aunt Lindsay said they had some blow-out fight over a girl. Pa and

Jericho were both so hardheaded, Aunt Lindsay said, it was just the last straw. Jericho took off, took the girl with him, and never came back. Grandma Anne used to get a post card from Jericho once a year on Christmas, and that was it."

Noah seemed to consider Luke's words for a minute.

"That's a sad story," Noah concluded.

Luke sat up, pinning Noah with a hard glare.

"I am trying to draw a parallel here, Noah. Pa was the dominant twin, just like you are. I imagine he was as much of a pain in the ass as you, too."

"And this is your business because…?" Noah snapped.

"It's my business if you drive off a member of this family. I don't know what you did to make Finn so mad, but you'd better undo it, pronto," Luke told him.

"I can't undo what I don't understand," Noah said, rising to his feet. Luke stood, shaking his head.

"He's not just going to wait around forever, looking at you like you're the only star in the sky. You have to talk to him, figure out what's going on. I want this settled before you all head to St. Louis."

Noah grunted and turned, shifting with a smooth leap and landing in his bear form. Luke winced, knowing that such a showy shift was very painful. Noah strode off without pause, though there was a limp in his step. Luke just scoffed, thinking that the moment summed up Noah Beran just perfectly.

THREE

Noah Beran shifted in the cramped airplane seat, trying to concentrate on the open laptop screen before him. The voices of his parents and brothers rose and ebbed all around him, soaking into his consciousness despite the fact that he had headphones in, music playing softly.

He lifted the arm rest between himself and the empty seat next to him, glad at least that his parents had bought out the first class section of the flight from Billings to St. Louis. It was a paltry gesture, considering the outlandish demands that his father had recently been making. At least he could spread out a little during the flight, get some work done. It also gave Noah the ability to continue putting off a long-overdue conversation with his twin brother Finn.

That conversation would happen, there was no avoiding it forever. But in aftermath of the Alphas' Council decree that all eligible Berserker bears would be taking mates, it was easy for Noah to slip away, seeking solitude. The first big social event to encourage mating, a huge barn dance hosted at his parents' Red Lodge home, had taken the heat off Noah for a solid week.

And now they were in the air, traveling to a second huge mixer, another set of Alpha families, more eligible women, and, if the universe was merciful, another open bar where Noah could forget the whole ridiculous scenario.

Noah looked around the cabin at his family: his mother and father seated at the back, having what appeared to be a heated discussion. No doubt Genny Beran was trying to talk her mate into something more moderate and reasonable, whatever the topic might be, and Josiah was resisting will all his willpower.

Gavin and Finn were half-standing in their respective rows across the aisle from Noah, chatting amiably over the seats. As the two brothers who lived closest to home, they saw each other much more often than any of the rest of the Beran men.

Cameron's big feet stuck out a couple of rows ahead of Noah. He was lying down, no doubt dealing with extreme nausea. Cam had been airsick, seasick, and carsick since birth, something Noah found funnier and funnier as Cameron grew bigger and more dominant with each passing year. A big, brawny bear shifter looking green around the gills was funny as hell, especially to his equally big, brawny Berserker brothers.

Noah blinked, his gaze returning to his laptop screen. He scrolled through a dozen more photos of his last assignment, a lengthy stay in Libya with the goal of capturing what his editor jokingly called 'truly heart-wrenching moments on film'. Noah had worked for the Tribune for nearly a decade now, starting at the very bottom shooting B-reel on fluff pieces, stories about firefighters saving cats and ladies who did extreme couponing. Now the Tribune just assigned him a location in the world and sent him off, knowing that he would return with the goods. A long, touching story about poverty and absolution, vivid color photographs of sacred cultural events. Noah knew what the editors loved; he had several boxes of journalism trophies sitting in the living room of his near-empty LA apartment, proving his capability and value.

Noah closed his eyes and leaned his head back, holding in an angry sigh. He let the music in his headphones wash over him, the sounds of his favorite Arcade Fire album lulling him. He hadn't been sleeping well recently. No, scratch that. He hadn't been sleeping well for the last year or so, since his Laos assignment took a really bad turn.

Pushing away the dark thoughts that threatened to rise,

Noah frowned when he felt the seat next to him depress. He opened his eyes, already knowing what he would see: himself, reflected exactly. Who needed a mirror when you had an identical twin around?

"Finn," Noah said, keeping his voice measured. He pulled out his ear buds, reaching out to close his laptop.

"Big brother," Finn intoned with a smirk.

"Only by seven minutes," Noah said, relaxing as he slipped into the cadence of brotherhood he'd known since birth. Noah looked Finn over, noting that his brother had trimmed his dark hair close to the scalp. Noah preferred to keep his very short on the sides but longer on the top, letting the sun-streaked chestnut locks grow into a stylish, tousled look that women seemed to like.

They had the same broad, dark brows, the same finely chiseled nose and firm jaw. They both had broad, flashing smiles that ladies loved, especially when Noah and Finn were sitting side by side. Though Noah had spent countless hours under the intense equatorial sun, he and Finn shared the same deeply tan skin. They were tall and muscular, less broad than their brawny brothers, their arms and legs and hands more elegantly wrought than Luke or Gavin or Wyatt. On smaller men, they might seem wiry, but Noah and Finn were simply lean.

And then there was Noah's best feature, and therefore Finn's too: the vivid blue-green eyes, just the color of the ocean before a storm, pupils rimmed in a hint of canary yellow. When Noah was happy, his eyes drew people in flocks. In anger, they drove away the same, flashing with fury. In matters of expression and of the heart, for the men in the Beran family, it was all in the eyes.

Noah closed his eyes briefly, wondering at the genetic anomaly that was not just his twin brother, but his whole family.

"You look wiped out. Surely not a result of flying, since you're the world traveler of the family," Finn said, cocking his head. Noah opened his eyes and felt his own head cant to the side, mirroring his brother's movements. Another annoying twin trait that neither of them seemed able to shake, no matter how far apart they might be in distance.

"I haven't been sleeping well," Noah said, straightening out of his mirrored pose.

"Man, ever since Pa told us that the Alphas' Council has basically married us off, I've been tossing and turning nonstop."

"Really? Sharing a room with you for the last few nights, I hardly noticed," Noah said. He didn't have to worry that Finn would miss his sarcasm; unlike every other person in the world, his twin read his tone correctly every time.

"Hey, it's not my fault that Ma turned your room into a pottery studio. You're the one who didn't come home for two years straight."

Noah couldn't miss the blatant accusation in his brother's tone, though it might have sounded friendly and casual to anyone else listening. He gave Finn the ghost of a smile, shaking his head.

"I've been busy," Noah replied with a shrug.

"You've missed a lot," Finn informed him, settling back into his seat and turning his gaze forward.

"Yeah? Like what? Cows are born, horses die, the US Presidents embarrass the country..." Noah waved a dismissive hand.

"Yeah. Because nothing interesting can happen in Red Lodge. The only things worth being present for are out there, in the great beyond," Finn said, flipping his hand just as Noah had.

"Finn..."

"Don't worry about it, Noe," Finn said, making Noah cringe at the use of his childhood nickname. "We all know that you're too busy and important to come home. Or email, or call. Or even text. It's not like Ma bought you a satellite phone, for the specific purpose of being able to contact us anywhere in the world, anytime."

"That phone died. About four sat phones ago, actually. In any event, I go long periods of time without any electricity for indoor lights, much less plugging in a phone and a laptop. Libya is too busy fighting for freedom from governmental oppression. Some people have bigger things to worry about."

Finn snorted.

"Right. You're a ground-breaker, an adventurer, saving the world one Tribune article at a time. And here the rest of us are, just sitting around taking it easy."

"I didn't say that," Noah snapped.

"You don't say much of anything these days. I hear more from Luke than I do from you, and he's been fighting a war. Literally."

"We all have to go our own way," Noah said.

"Yeah. Your way is high-flying, fast living, and mine is boring and meaningless. I get it."

Noah looked over to find that his brother was once again in the same position as he was. Arms crossed, jaw tense, staring straight ahead as if to burn holes in the seats before them.

"Noah!" his mother called. Noah actually sagged in his seat from relief. He really didn't want this fight with Finn, and now that it had started, he didn't know how to end it. Was he supposed to apologize for living his life, leaving Red Lodge behind? It seemed insane.

"Duty calls," Noah said, rising and pushing past Finn into the aisle. His father had moved up front to talk with Gavin, so Noah dropped into the vacant seat next to his mother.

"Ma'am," Noah answered. His mother gave him a soft smile and put her dainty hand over his. She was always touching him when he was home, as if she was unsure whether or not he was real.

"Now, listen. About this mixer we're heading to," Ma said, giving him a searching look.

"Ah, yes. The great city of St. Louis. How it beckons," Noah said, giving his words a Shakespearean cast.

"I want you to give it a chance, okay? I've lined up something special for you."

Noah raised a brow.

"And what could that possibly be? A tour of the Arch, perhaps?"

Ma laughed and shook her head, refusing to take his words as unkind.

"No, better than that. I found you a journalist," she said.

"A journalist."

"Yes. The daughter of the Krall Alpha."

"She's like a TV weather girl or something?" Noah asked, suspicious.

"No, she covers politics. In Washington D.C.," his mother replied, giving him a firm look.

"Politics, huh?" Noah was touched that his mother had thought of him at all, seeing as how she had five other sons and most of them came home once in a while.

"Yes. Her name is Abby, and she's supposed to be very pretty and very smart. Your Aunt Susan knows the Krall clan pretty well, and when she told me about Abby, I thought of you."

Noah had less than zero interest in being set up by his mother and Aunt Susan, but he wouldn't be rude. At least this way he might have someone interesting to talk to at the mixer.

"Thanks, Ma," he said, leaning over to give her a hug.

"I want you to keep Finn close during the mixer," she stipulated, pointing a stern finger at him.

"To keep me out of trouble?" Noah asked. A joke… mostly.

Ma gave him an unfathomable expression, concern evident in her gaze.

"It's better for both of you when you're together, not that either of you has the sense to know it," she scolded.

"Ah, so I'm the one taking care of Finn this time," Noah teased. His mother rolled her eyes and sighed.

"Just do as I ask for once?"

"Anything for you, Ma," Noah promised with a chuckle.

The overhead lights went up suddenly, the seatbelt sign dinging throughout the cabin.

"In that case, you can carry my bag once we get to the baggage claim," she said, patting his hand. "Now buckle up!"

Noah repressed the urge to roll his eyes as he fastened his seatbelt and waited for the plane to descend into St. Louis.

FOUR

Charlotte Krall stopped in the parking lot, a hundred yards from the stone archway of the Hilton's Grand Hall , eyeing the words *St. Louis Union Station* emblazoned over the entrance. The site of the huge Berserker party they were attending this evening… if Charlotte could make herself go inside, that was.

"You've never been in here?" Abby asked. Charlotte licked her lips as she glanced over at her stunning brunette cousin, shaking her head.

"Never," Charlotte admitted.

"It's lovely. You'll like it," Abby announced, all confidence as she linked her arm with Charlotte's and pulled her cousin along.

"Wait, wait!" Charlotte said, resisting. "I just… how do I look, Abby?"

Abby pulled back with an expression of mock-seriousness, examining Charlotte from head to toe. Abby held up her fingers, ticking off Charlotte's physical attributes as she went.

"Let's see… five foot seven inches of hourglass curves, check. Waist-length ash blonde hair, styled like a lion's mane… check. Sexy fifties-style red dress that fits in all the right places without showing off too much…. check. Killer black heels and purse… double check. Your makeup is on point, your whole thing is working for me here," Abby said, waving a hand to indicate Charlotte's person. "What's the deal?"

Charlotte sighed.

"We're about to walk into THE social event of the fall season, where every single Berserker is waiting. Including the guy your father is determined to set you up with," Charlotte said. "The one who I have to bamboozle into falling for me so that he doesn't accidentally out you to your parents. And look at you! It's not going to be easy."

Abby pursed her lips and looked down at herself, her slender curves dressed in a stylish white pant suit and bright red heels. Eyes twinkling, she gave Abby a casual shrug.

"I can't help that I'm stunningly beautiful," Abby teased. "And with the personality to match…"

She linked arms with Charlotte once more, pulling her toward the entrance.

"Well, all the guys in here are going to be awfully disappointed when you don't go home with a single one. If they knew that you batted for other team, they'd be so sad," Charlotte told Abby. Abby laughed and squeezed Charlotte's arm.

"Not as sad as my parents would be, I assure you." Abby's expression sobered. "Thank you for doing this for me, Charlotte. I'm not ready to tell my parents that I'm only interested in women. I think it might kill my mother."

"I think you should have a little more faith in her, Abs," Charlotte said, squeezing Abby's arm right back.

"Maybe. In any event, they don't know, and I doubt that right now is the time to tell them. My mother's got me all set up with some guy…"

Abby's voice trailed off as they stepped into Union Station.

"Whoa…" Abby said.

The place was massive; arched ivory and gold ceilings soared a hundred feet high, and the space was as big as half a football field. Sweeping arches done in hints of deep green and teak, frolicked with the Station's gilded style, mosaics and murals blending into an eye-popping homage to Art Deco. At one end stood an immense stained-glass window picturing three beautiful women all holding leisurely poses. At the other end of the hall was a gleaming marble bar, tuxedoed bartenders already in motion, serving drinks to the early arrivals. One area of the hall held a small sea of ruby-red velour chairs, chaises, and couches; another area was cleared out for dancing, complete with a band and a high-tech DJ setup.

"This is something," Charlotte uttered, hurrying herself inside as she realized that others were entering the hall just behind her.

"They've changed it a lot since that last time I was here," Abby said.

Charlotte spotted Jared and Lindsay Krall, Abby's parents, in a cluster of middle-aged Berserkers. Probably the very men who had made the decision to force mateships on all eligible Berserkers of age, regardless of desire to mate. The Alphas' Council was sponsoring the event, but the Kralls had been in charge of all the details. Already Lindsay had spotted Abby and Charlotte and was waving them over to join their conversation.

"Let's get a drink before Mom drags us into whatever dull conversation she's in," Abby said, grabbing Charlotte's hand and towing her across the hall toward the bar. The room was starting to fill up now, more and more groups of shifters arriving. The second that the drinks were in their hands, Abby spotted someone across the room and perked up. "There she is!"

"There who is?" Charlotte asked, sipping her gin and tonic.

"The only other lesbian Berserker that exists, I think," Abby said, tilting her head across the room at a tall, athletic redhead who threw her head back to let out a throaty laugh. "Marleigh Kinnear, from Vermont. She's quite sexy, isn't she?"

"She really is!" Charlotte agreed. "You'd better go talk to her. Maybe you two can work out something clever, eh?"

"Hmmm," Abby murmured, downing the rest of her whiskey sour in one long gulp. "I think I'll have to take your advice, cousin."

With that Abby set off, shoulders back and head held high. Charlotte almost giggled at the way that several men stopped to stare at Abby as she stalked across the room. She watched as

Abby leaned down and said something to Marleigh, who laughed, and soon Abby and Marleigh were settled on one of the chaise lounges together, deep in conversation. Charlotte sighed and leaned back against the gleaming pearly marble of the bar, just soaking in the beauty of the place.

"And who do you belong to?" came a deep voice from behind Charlotte. She spun in place to find a silver-haired man, dressed in a dark suit. She couldn't place him, since almost every older male here was silver-haired and dressed in dark attire.

"The Kralls," Charlotte told him. "Charlotte Krall, niece of Alpha Jared Krall."

"Josiah Beran," the man replied, thrusting out a hand to her. She shook it, noticing that his grip was surprisingly weak for his size. The man was almost six and a half feet tall and looked to be in fine health, but his hand shook when he released her.

"Beran... Oh, you and your mate threw the first mixer! Abby said it was lovely," Charlotte said.

"You didn't attend," Josiah said. A statement, not a question. As if he would have remembered her. The fine hairs on Charlotte's neck rose as she wondered to herself whether Josiah might actually be *flirting* with her. Just at that moment, the lights in the Grand Hall dimmed, making the gathering feel more intimate. Overhead, spotlights painted the gold-and-cream ceiling in vibrant shades of mauve and the seven-piece band started playing "Jump, Jive, and Wail".

Charlotte looked at Josiah Beran, clearing her throat and speaking up to make herself heard over the band and the chatter of the other Berserkers.

"Uh, no... My father is not an Alpha. I'm here supporting my cousin Abby, Jared and Lindsay's daughter," Charlotte said, nodding to her cousin. Josiah turned and took a long look at Abby before shrugging and returning his attention to Charlotte. Charlotte was surprised, because for most men Abby was too beautiful and engaging to be so easily dismissed.

"Come with me," he said, reaching out and grasping Charlotte by the wrist. Charlotte hesitated at first, throughly put off by his gruff, demanding demeanor, but she thought it would be impolite to physically resist him. So she allowed herself to be towed along, her eyes growing wide when she realized that he was heading for the dance floor.

Surely this older Alpha didn't intend to actually dance with her? Charlotte's pulse rate rose, and she flushed with distaste. Perhaps Josiah had dismissed Abby in favor of Charlotte because he sensed that she was more gentle, an easier target for... well, whatever it was he had in mind?

Josiah pulled up short on one side of the dance floor, glaring down at a striking younger man who lounged alone, watching the dance floor. One glance between them made Charlotte certain that they were related; the younger man's dark good looks and bright blue eyes echoed Josiah's too closely to be anything but a blood relative.

"This is Charlotte," Josiah told the man, a look passing between them. "Charlotte, this is my son Finn."

Finn rose from his seat, six and a half feet of tall, dark, and jaw-droppingly handsome. He wore a slick black suit and tie with a crisp white shirt, all perfectly tailored to fit his lean, muscular frame. His dark mahogany hair was close-cropped but stylish, his face all stony angles under dark brows, and he was deeply tanned.

Charlotte opened her mouth, but Finn simply held out his hand.

"Nice to meet you, Charlotte. Would you like to dance?" he asked.

Charlotte's mouth dropped open when Josiah stepped up behind her and gave her a light but unmissable push, making her stumble against Finn. Finn caught her with ease, a dazzling smile lighting up his face when his hands closed around her upper arms. Charlotte shivered at his touch, a distinctive fire-and-ice sizzle flaring over her skin.

Charlotte looked up at Finn, a wavering smile on her lips.

"This doesn't bode well for dancing, does it?" she joked.

"I wouldn't worry too much," he said, his eyes sparkling with mischief. Up close, she noticed that they were the most beautiful shade of green blue, an oceanic tint rimming a thin band of vivid yellow around his irises.

The band was playing a mid-tempo tune Charlotte recognized, something easy for her to catch onto. Finn led her out onto the dance floor with practiced ease, settling one big hand on her waist and another on her shoulder. Charlotte did the same, butterflies fluttering in her stomach.

Finn gave her a big smile as he led her through the movements, a simple box step. The expression on his face and the genuine happiness in his eyes made it easy for Charlotte to relax and enjoy herself. It wasn't often that she interacted with someone as good-looking as Finn Beran, and when she did it was rarely a comfortable experience. Men like Finn weren't littering the sidewalks of St. Louis, and the ones Charlotte did encounter were usually far too full of themselves for her taste. So far, Finn had proved quite the surprise.

"You're really good at this!" Charlotte said, grinning up at Finn.

"My mother taught all of us to dance," he said, a dimple flashing in his cheek.

"Your brothers and sisters?"

"Brothers. All six of us."

"Six of you! Gracious!" Charlotte declared. She couldn't imagine six Finns running around the world, breaking hearts and causing trouble.

"Oh yeah. She made all of us learn by seventh grade, gave her a couple years' break between lessons," he said. "She told us all that it would help us get girlfriends, which was the only way any of us would go along with it."

"Did it? Help, I mean," Charlotte said.

"Not in middle school, it didn't. Not for me, anyway."

Charlotte gave him a doubtful glance, thinking that he'd probably been quite popular in seventh grade. They danced and chatted for almost half an hour, keeping topics light and neutral. Charlotte found that she had to lead the conversation as much as Finn had to lead her in dancing; he was very sweet and dashing, but a hair more reserved than what she normally liked in a man. He also kept glancing over her shoulder into the far corner of the room. Charlotte had the distinct impression that he was keeping tabs on someone, and she couldn't help but assume that it was some woman who'd caught his eye. For all she knew, Finn had a girlfriend already.

After a few more minutes, Charlotte sighed and stepped back.

"I'm going to go to the restroom and then find my way to the bar. Maybe we can take another turn a little later?" she asked.

"Sure thing," Finn said, giving her hand a soft squeeze before releasing her. He really was every inch the true gentleman, and if she ever met his mother she'd be certain to compliment her on raising such a man. Maybe Finn was worth pursuing, after all.

Charlotte took a couple of steps toward the bathroom and looked back, only to find Finn heading off toward the far corner, the spot he'd been so closely monitoring as they danced. She shook her head and sighed, making her way to the ladies' room to freshen up.

FIVE

Once she'd hit the bar for another gin and tonic, she decided that it was high time to find Abby. Some chaperone Charlotte was, running off to dance with handsome guys instead of protecting Abby from their inevitable advances. After ordering a drink for Abby, Charlotte spotted her at a table in the same far corner where she'd seen Finn heading...

Speak of the devil, Finn was actually sitting at a table with Abby, leaning in close to hear something she was saying. For some reason he'd donned a dark gray fedora, tipped at a stylish angle. Though Charlotte generally disliked hats on men, Finn managed to look even more dashing in it.

Charlotte looked around for Marleigh, the beautiful redhead that had caught Abby's eye earlier, but didn't see her anywhere. Charlotte headed for her cousin, feeling doubly bad that she hadn't even been able to protect her from the one man Charlotte had flirted with all night. As Charlotte watched, Finn leaned close to Abby again and said something that made her chuckle and roll her eyes. The avid interest was plain on Finn's face, and Charlotte groaned aloud.

Sucking in a deep breath, Charlotte decided that she was going to insert herself into the situation and lay the charm on thick. She saw a buxom blonde a few tables away, sitting on a handsome redheaded man's lap. He was staring at the blonde in complete thrall, and Charlotte took a little inspiration from the other woman.

Arriving at Abby and Finn's table, she gave them both a dazzling smile.

"There you both are," Charlotte said, keeping her expression bright. "Abby, I got you a drink. I saw your friend Marleigh at the bar, she wanted you to come say hi."

Sliding the drink across the table, Charlotte gave her cousin a heavy glance. Abby popped up and grabbed the drink with a grin.

"I'd better go say hi," Abby said, escaping.

When Finn made to rise and follow, Charlotte set her drink down and skirted the table, putting her hand on his shoulder to keep him in place.

"And where are you going? I thought we could spend a little more time together," Charlotte purred.

Finn's eyes raked over her from head to toe, one brow rising. He bit his lip for a second, the movement so sensual as to almost be a come-on, and he gave her a considering smile. That dimple flashed in his cheek again, and Charlotte's heart fluttered. Looking down at Finn, she couldn't believe how much different their chemistry was now than it had been just a handful of minutes before.

Finn reached out and snagged her wrist, brushing his thumb over the sensitive skin there. His eyes glinted with something much darker than before. Though their contact was less now than it had been during their dance, something she saw in him now, some hunger, made her bold.

"I suppose a little more time is due…" Finn said. He looked up at her with an anticipatory gleam in his eyes, and Charlotte felt her body respond to him, tightening and heating.

Biting her lip to mimic his earlier expression, Charlotte wrapped one arm around his neck and slid down onto his lap. If Finn was the least bit surprised, he didn't show it. Finn adjusted his position, pressing the roundness of her ass against his fully-alert cock for the barest moment. Charlotte blushed, but didn't demur.

"So how did you meet my cousin?" Charlotte asked the first thing that came to mind, blushing harder at her lack of finesse.

"My mother put us together. We're both journalists, so she thought we'd have something in common," he said.

"Is that so? I wouldn't have pegged you for a journalist. You seem more the grounded type," Charlotte said, though now she was second-guessing herself.

"I get to travel the world and catch the best stories," Finn said with a shrug. "I win awards, I make good money. There's no downside really."

A shadow flitted over his face at the last, but it was gone in an instant.

"I'm surprised you didn't lead with that earlier," Charlotte said, wondering at the fact that she'd had to guide the conversation before. Finn seemed much more relaxed now, in his element, and completely at ease with himself.

"I don't want to bowl you over or anything," he teased. His words were joking, but there was a definitive cockiness to them now. Charlotte furrowed her brow, confused.

"You said you lived a simple life, before," she said slowly. Finn shrugged and gave her another closed-mouth smile, looking like nothing so much as a lion on the prowl. He tilted his head to the side, the warmth of his breath skittering over the exposed nape of her neck. Charlotte suppressed another shiver, now beginning to regret her decision to sit on Finn's lap. She wasn't that sort of girl, and this is what she got for her intrigues.

"Did I? I'm remarkably modest sometimes," he said.

"It seems that way," Charlotte replied, the words out of her mouth before she could stop herself.

"Yes, well. Being humble is pretty boring, if you ask me. I'd much rather prove myself interesting..." He paused, as if trying to remember her name.

"It's Charlotte," she snapped. Mortified, she used his shoulder to push herself up out of his lap. "I can't believe you already forgot my name!"

"Charlotte..." he said, seeming to savor the word. He grabbed her wrist again, holding her captive before she could flee. "Charlotte, there's something you don't understand..."

"I'll just bet there is, Finn Beran!" Charlotte wrenched her hand from his and spun on her heel, gasping as she smashed into a very angry... Finn?

"What the..." Charlotte looked at Finn, and then looked behind her. One was thunderously angry, the other seemed quite amused.

"Noah, for fuck's sake!" Angry Finn shouted, drawing the attention of several onlookers. "What the hell have you done now?"

Abby appeared at Charlotte's elbow, drawing her back a step.

"Noah?" Charlotte gaped.

"We're twins," Finn explained, looking downright apologetic.

"Oh!" was all Charlotte could manage. Finn's identical twin gave her a smirk and took off his fedora, revealing his hair; his tousled locks were much longer than Finn's, cut in a fashionable style that made Charlotte's fingers itch to touch him, see what texture the dark strands held.

She turned to Noah with a scowl, intending to scold him but uncertain how to do so. The smirk that played on his lips made her flush with anger and embarrassment, but before she could take him to task Josiah Beran and Jared Krall appeared. Both Alphas were eyeing Abby and Noah with great interest, and Charlotte could see her cousin go pale.

"Looks as if you all are getting along just fine," Josiah said, turning his gaze to Charlotte and Finn, who stood only inches apart.

"That we are," Noah drawled, earning punishing glances from Charlotte, Abby, and Finn.

"Dad..." Abby started, but Josiah cut her off.

"Jared here has arranged for Abby and Charlotte to take you boys out on the town. Go see the Arch, or go to a club, whatever it is you kids do around here."

Abby and Charlotte exchanged a look, knowing very well that those were certainly not on their list of must-see attractions, but both held their tongues. A brief glance at the twins showed Finn's discomfort and Noah's seeming pleasure at the arrangement.

"Well, since that's settled," Jared Krall said, raising a brow at Abby and Charlotte as if challenging them to derail his plans. "Ladies, the mixer will be over in less than an hour, and neither of you has been introduced to the Risal or Knoer clans. Abby, your mother wanted me to drag you away from the Berans for a bit."

Charlotte and Abby both gave the Beran men stiff yet polite smiles as they excused themselves to follow their Alpha. They dropped a few paces behind him for a little privacy.

"Abby, you have to tell your father that you and Noah don't suit," Charlotte demanded. "This is already getting out of hand."

"I don't see a problem," Abby said with a shrug. "So we have to go out to dinner with two very handsome men. It's not the worst fate in the world."

"Abby! You're leading everyone on, Josiah Beran and your father included. It's not right!"

Abby grabbed Charlotte's hand, clasping it in her own, and gave her a very serious look.

"Charlotte, just because the Berans aren't right for me doesn't mean they're not right for you," she explained.

Charlotte made a squawk of protest, unsettled.

"Abby, we aren't here to match make for me! I'm only here to defend your interests, remember?"

"And I'm doing the same for you. Both those men looked at you like you're the best thing since sliced bread, and I'm not going to out myself to my father to prevent you from going out with sexy, available men who find you attractive. You're talking crazy right now."

"Abby!" Charlotte cried, but Jared Krall was already turning to introduce them to another group of eligible Berserker males.

Charlotte shut up and pasted on a smile, determined not to let her Alpha down. Still, she shot a long look at Abby, letting her cousin know that they were not yet finished discussing the topic of her deceptive, match-making intentions.

SIX

Noah drummed his fingertips on the lacquered wood tabletop, soaking in the brass-and-oak decor of the Lafayette Square wine bar that the Krall girls chose as the spot for their forcefully-arranged double date. Though Noah had originally intended to catch the first flight back to Los Angeles, seeing as he had a deadline and mountains of work to do before he could possibly meet it, but some devilish part of him made him stay. Just to see what a disaster their double date would be, he told himself.

Noah felt the rhythmic vibration on the table of another set of fingertips, drumming in the same beat, and he slid an annoyed gaze over to his twin.

"Do you have to do that?" Noah asked, raising a brow.

Finn looked down at his own hand, giving Noah a shrug in response. Finn hadn't even been aware of his own mimicry, Noah was certain. It was that way with them, always had been.

The waiter arrived with a nice bottle of Syrah that Noah had selected, presenting and uncorking it before leaving them with a glass each. Noah and Finn both sampled the wine, Noah swirling and sniffing first while Finn just took a sip and gave a pleasurable sigh.

"Pretty good," Finn said, his gaze drawing up to the doorway, checking once more to see if the Kralls had arrived. They were fifteen minutes late by now, and Finn despised tardiness. Before Noah could reply, the door opened and Charlotte and Abby stepped inside.

"Holy shit..." Finn muttered, and Noah couldn't help but agree. Abby was dressed casually in jeans and a filmy white top, dressed up just enough for the bar's standards. Charlotte, though...

Charlotte wore a pastel-green dress that clung to every magnificent curve, emphasizing her incredible body while covering her from elbow to knee. A white belt marked her waist, making her considerable breasts and hips even more enticing. White heels gave her stride a feminine flair, her hips swaying as she spotted Noah and Finn and made her way to the table. Abby trailed behind with a distinctly displeased expression, though Noah only looked at her for half a second before returning to her sexier, blonder cousin. He noticed that her wide sapphire-hued eyes were lined with kohl, a smoky look that emphasized the perfect proportions of her nose, lips, and cheeks.

"Gentlemen," Charlotte said as she reached the table, setting down her white clutch across from Noah. A shadow flitted across Finn's face before he jumped up and pulled out Abby's seat, forcing Noah to rise and do the same for Charlotte.

"Sorry we're late," Charlotte said as she settled down at the table, casting a glance at her cousin.

"No problem," Finn said, his tone verging on overeager. Noah spread his hand out on the table, a silent gesture to his brother: *take it down a notch*.

"We went ahead and ordered a bottle of Syrah," Noah said.

"Thank god," Abby said. "May I?"

"Of course," Noah replied, clearing his throat. As awkward as he'd imagined this to be, it was certainly more so now.

"So..." Charlotte began, pursing her lips as Abby filled their wine glasses nearly to the brim. "Finn, tell me a little about yourself. I know we danced for a while at the mixer, but I didn't find out that much about you."

"I'm a high school teacher," Finn supplied. "I mainly teach

English, but I also do some computer lit classes and yearbook, whatever the school needs."

"Very cool. Abby actually studied English Literature at Mizzou, didn't you Abs?"

"That I did," Abby replied, taking a long sip of her wine. There was a long pause before Noah leaned in to fill the silence.

"And you, Charlotte? What did you study?" he asked.

"I have a bachelor's degree in nursing," Charlotte said.

"Ah! What a candy striper you must make," Noah joked. Charlotte's mouth pulled into a tight line, and he could see that he'd already managed to offend her. Not surprising, since he was generally kind of an asshole, but he was a little disappointed in himself. He hadn't even made it ten minutes without putting Charlotte out.

"Charlotte works at the Children's Hospital," Abby informed him. "She works in the ICU, dealing with really, really sick kids that might die without constant care."

Noah was at a loss for a long moment, giving Finn the opportunity to jump in.

"That's incredible. It must take a lot of guts to do that," Finn said, earning a soft smile from Charlotte.

"Yeah, sometimes it does," she said with a shrug. "I'm not traveling the world or anything, but it's satisfying when a patient makes it through a really tough time."

Noah, Finn, and Abby all nodded.

"That sounds like a pretty demanding job," Noah acknowledged, thinking of a med student he'd dated years ago. "You must be at the hospital all the time, away from home a lot."

Finn snorted.

"Say the man that hasn't made it home to Montana in almost three years. When is the last time that you were at that apartment of yours for more than forty-eight hours, globe trotter?" he asked.

Noah nodded, conceding his point.

"It's been a long time. I work abroad, I vacation abroad," he said, waving a dismissive hand.

"You must have been to some really exotic locations," Charlotte said, moving the conversation along. Noah liked that she kept things light, that she seemed to care for everyone's comfort. It made sense for a nurse to worry about others like that, of course.

"Well... yeah. On my vacations, I've gone to all kinds of places. Greece, Argentina, Thailand, New Zealand. If there's something to be seen, I want to see it," Noah said.

"You should see his passport," Finn said. "Bursting with stamps."

Noah shot his twin a quelling look, but said nothing. He eyed Abby for a long moment, suddenly realizing how quiet she'd been this whole time. Abby merely arched a brow at him before turning her attention back to her cousin.

"And for work? Surely a traveling journalist sees a lot of cool stuff," Charlotte said.

"Uhhh," Noah said, rubbing his neck. "Well, I mostly report on political power clashes, so it's not especially scenic. I go where the action is, and I spend half my time trying not to get blown up in the process."

Charlotte and Abby both looked surprised, while Finn just gave him a brief smirk. The waiter came around, and Abby selected a pricey bottle of rosé champagne for their next round. After a flurry of removal and resetting of the table, the champagne arrived in a silver ice bucket. Once their flutes were filled, they all clinked their glasses together. The genteelness of the moment nearly made Noah laugh out loud, thinking of some of the less civilized drinking experiences he'd had in the last year. Hot moonshine out of a flask in Tripoli, fermented coconut wine on a beach in San Juan, liquor and snake's blood shots in Thailand...

"Do you live in Billings like Finn does?" Charlotte asked, breaking into his thoughts.

"No, I moved to L.A. a few years ago. A friend of mine owns a building close to the Tribune offices, and he looks after my place while I'm away," Noah said.

"And you, Finn? Are you a traveler like your brother?" Charlotte asked.

Finn looked distinctly uncomfortable, so much so that Noah cut in before he could respond.

"We should get some appetizers, don't you think?" Noah said, grabbing the menus off the table and passing them around. Finn gave him a heated glance, neither angry nor appreciative, and then buried his nose in the menu.

SEVEN

Two plates of finger food and several bottles of wine later, the conversation was considerably more relaxed... not to mention more interesting, in Noah's opinion.

"Abby," Charlotte said, pointing dramatically at her cousin, "Is not a *prude*, she just has *standards*."

"I have standards," Noah said, giving her a skeptical glance. "I'm way more picky than my brother."

Noah nudged Finn in the ribs, earning a hateful glare from his twin.

"If one of us is picky, it's me," Finn retorted. "I haven't been traveling the world, sleeping with god knows what kind of women."

This elicited a snort from Abby, who looked interested for the first time in over an hour.

"What kinds of women?" Abby asked Noah.

"Uh, no one wants to hear about that," Charlotte interrupted, turning to mouth a reproach at Abby. "Maybe we need some more wine!"

'Whoa, whoa," Finn said, grabbing Charlotte's hand across the table before she could flag down the waiter for another bottle. "Take it easy. We've had more than a bottle each."

Noah looked at the two women, taking in Charlotte's over-the-top antics and Abby's slouching crankiness, and wondered what they hell they were hiding. It was more than clear to him, even with a whole bottle of wine in his stomach, that Charlotte was covering for Abby. But what the secret could possibly be, he couldn't guess. It was clear that Abby was only here because her father had forced her to come, that much was obvious. That was no reason for Charlotte's desperate bids to draw his and Finn's attention away from her cousin, though.

"So, Abby. What's your deal?" Noah asked suddenly, leaning forward on his elbows as he stared the darker-haired cousin down.

"What do you mean? She's fine!" Charlotte declared.

"She wants to leave. Do you have a boyfriend or something? A human?" Noah asked, watching the woman's face contort with anger.

Abby drew herself up, pushing her chair back, and threw her napkin down with a huff.

"Ladies' room, Char?" she intoned, staring daggers at Charlotte.

"Uh, right," Charlotte said, rising and clearing her throat. "Right back, guys."

Noah and Finn watched in silence as the women disappeared into the back hallway.

"Are we going to end up in a fist fight?" Finn asked as soon as they were out of earshot.

Noah raised his eyebrows, surprised at his twin's bluntness.

"Not if I have any choice in the matter. You have a killer right hook, if I remember correctly," Noah said.

"So, what, then? We let Charlotte choose between us?"

"That's the way of the animal kingdom, brother."

Finn gave Noah a deadly glare, shaking his head.

"That's not fair of you. You're going to stay in the game even though you're not playing for keeps," Finn said, looking bitter.

"Who says I'm not? And for that matter, who says you are?"

"You would sweep her off her feet, fuck her, and then leave for Cairo in the middle of the night," Finn said, matter-of-factly. He pinned Noah with a knowing look, making angry heat rise in Noah's cheeks.

"And you'd take her as a mate, right here on the table, huh?" Noah replied, running his fingertips around the rim of his wineglass, aiming his words to rile his brother.

"No, but at least I'd only be a few hours away. Something could blossom between us," Finn insisted.

"I'm not traveling for a while, as it happens," Noah said. He looked up at Finn's flushed face, knowing that the aggression he saw there was mirrored in his own expression.

"What are you talking about?" Finn asked, giving him a bored look.

"I'm a sabbatical. I've been setting up interviews with different news agencies, trying to get a cushy desk job."

Finn gave him an assessing glance before shaking his head.

"You're going to give up your life's passion to sit at a desk?" Finn laughed. "You won't make it a month."

"I'm serious, Finny. I've burned out. I'm going to do something else—"

"You are such a son of a bitch!" Finn declared, cutting off Noah's sentence. "You're just going to sweep in, be the charming twin, and scoop her up before I can have a chance. God, you haven't changed a bit, have you?"

"Hey, guys!" Charlotte called, approaching the table. "Uh, Abby's not feeling that well. I think she had a little too much to drink. She's going to get a cab home."

Noah kept his expression clear, but he was highly skeptical of Charlotte's excuses for her cousin. Finn rose to his feet, looking concerned.

"Should we escort you both home?" Finn asked, wincing when Noah stomped on Finn's foot under the table.

"I wasn't quite ready to call it a night. I mean, unless you guys are worn out…" Charlotte said. Something in her expression belied her words; Noah could tell that her invitation to keep partying was more of the same, covering up something about Abby. Still, he wouldn't deny himself the pleasure of Charlotte's company if she offered it.

"Finn's had the first dance… maybe I could have the next?"

Noah said, raking his gaze up and down Charlotte's thick curves, grinning when she blushed under his frank appreciation.

"Maybe both of you," Charlotte teased, her eyes growing wide after the words were out of her mouth. Her cheeks truly flamed pink now, but Noah wasn't going to let her take it back.

Could she really be interested in both men at once? Noah gave Finn a hungry look, smirking when Finn just shook his head and sighed in response.

"Only one way to find out, I guess," Noah said, signaling the waiter for the check. In moments they were paid up and following Charlotte outside, toward a club she claimed to enjoy. If she had any idea the kind of raunchy images that were in Noah's head, she would drop everything and run.

Lucky for Noah, Charlotte seemed more interested in her game of distraction than in reading his intentions. Lucky indeed…

EIGHT

The second that Charlotte stepped inside the darkened hallway leading into Club Baroque, she wondered if she was making a mistake. The music pulsed all around her, a persistent beat that seemed to make her very blood thrum with excitement. The wine made her feel warm and excited, happy and relaxed in a way she'd never been on previous visits to Club Baroque. The last time she'd come here was for a friend's bachelorette party, and Charlotte had spent the whole night sipping expensive bottled water in a VIP booth, watching out for all her drunk friends.

Not so, tonight. When the doors closed behind them, Finn grasped her hand and Noah touched the small of her back, both guiding her toward the packed dance floor. Beautiful, well-dressed people writhed in time with the music, and beautiful dancers stalked up and down high platforms adorning each wall.

"Do you need something to drink? Water?" Finn asked, leaning in to make himself heard over the booming music. His lips brushed her ear, and Charlotte bit her lip. She looked up at him, saw the earnestness in his expression, and nodded. A little water wouldn't hurt her right now, and it would definitely help her tomorrow.

Finn gave her a wink, pure sweetness, and made his way toward the bar. When Charlotte made to follow, Noah gripped her waist and pulled her toward the dance floor instead. She glanced up at him, saw the desire written plain on his handsome face, and melted a little bit.

She allowed Noah to lead her into the crush of dancers, let him tug her close as they both began to move to the music. Charlotte swayed her hips as Noah pressed against her, chest to chest. She tipped her head back, looking up into his beautiful turquoise eyes, licking her lips as her heart hammered in her chest in time with the music. She let her eyelids flutter closed, wondering if he would kiss her, ravish her mouth right here on the dance floor, but an icy sensation made her start.

Broad, warm hands touched her lower back as she opened her eyes, realizing that Finn had pressed a bottle of water into her hand. She let her head drop way back, looking up at his face and giving him an upside-down grin. Finn moved closer, pressing against her back just as Noah was pressed against her front, moving in perfect rhythm with his twin.

Charlotte paused for a moment, uncapping and downing the water before carelessly tossing the bottle onto the darkened floor. She was littering, but she was also way beyond caring.

Refreshed, she laid one hand on Noah's shoulder and reached the other back to caress Finn's neck, enjoying the heat of their bodies as they moved against her. She leaned her head back onto Finn's chest as he held her waist, half-supporting her. Hands trailed up and down her hips and ribs and arms, presumably Noah's. Charlotte wasn't sure, and she felt much to good to analyze.

A little voice in her head cried out, telling her that she was beyond the pale, that everyone in the club must think she was some kind of slut. She couldn't help herself, though. The way they were touching her, the press of their hardened bodies against her ass and thighs made her sigh with want. Noah and Finn were both fully erect, their expressions that of unabashed hunger, so Charlotte reasoned that they must be enjoying this as much as she was.

Charlotte was always a good girl, always a dutiful daughter, a benevolent nurse. In this moment, though, she saw herself reflected in Noah and Finn's gazes: a sexy bombshell, something they wanted to pleasure and devour. She wanted that, she wanted it so badly it nearly hurt. It had been over a year since her last one-night-stand, and suddenly she didn't want to wait another minute. She was tipsy and horny and ready, ready for the promises she saw written on Noah and Finn's faces.

Only... how was she supposed to choose between them? They were literally identically handsome, though she was fond of Noah's longer hair. She reached up and thrust her fingers into his damp, disheveled locks, loving how warm and soft his hair felt against her fingers. She could imagine herself tugging at those locks while he did unimaginably dirty things to her...

Then she looked up at Finn, thinking how caring and kind he was. He was all the things she looked for in a man, all the things she'd never found in such a pretty package before. He'd be a careful, thorough lover, taking care of her every want.

Finn wore a light gray dress shirt and a black tie with dark slacks, where Noah was dressed once again in a white shirt and black dress pants. Noah's shirt was unbuttoned at the collar, giving her a glimpse of smooth, tan skin. Finn cut such a dashing figure in his tie, though...

She looked between the two one last time and heaved a sigh. She arched her back, bringing her lips to Finn's ear.

"How am I supposed to choose one of you?" she asked, her tone pleading.

Finn stiffened against her, and she noticed that Noah mirrored him after a second. She raised her head and looked at Noah, who was engaging in some silent communication with Finn. For a moment, Charlotte actually wondered if they had some kind of twin telepathy. She giggled to herself, her lips twisting up in a smile.

Noah lowered his lips to her ear, his warm breath against her sensitive flesh making her shiver.

"You don't have to choose tonight, Charlotte. Do you want us both?" he asked.

Charlotte bit her lip, looking up at him. His expression was sincere, free of judgment. She nodded, and was rewarded when

Noah brushed his lips against her neck. Half a second later, Finn kissed her neck in the same spot on the other side, and Charlotte thought she might die from want.

"Be right back. Stay with Noah," Finn whispered. The wonderful heat of his body vanished, but Noah's arms encircled her waist and held her close. Charlotte swayed to the music, savoring Noah's strength as they moved together.

Finn returned after a few minutes, whispering in Noah's ear. Noah nodded and they both took her by the hand and led her out of the club.

NINE

Charlotte kept her eyes on Noah and Finn, loving the way they flanked her as they crossed the street. They walked into a plush hotel lobby, bypassing the check-in desk. Charlotte looked up at Finn, her gaze questioning, as they stepped into a gleaming brass elevator.

Finn leaned down and pressed his lips gently to hers. When he withdrew, he placed a plastic keycard in her hand. She looked at Noah, who gave her a wink. They rode the elevator in silence for a minute, and before she knew it they were standing outside the door of room 315.

Charlotte glanced at Noah once more, appreciating his smile of encouragement. Taking a deep breath, she slid the keycard into the slot and opened the door, leading the way inside. The room was beautiful, all done in blush pink and ivory and gold, but Charlotte hardly noticed the decor. The only thing that caught her eye was the king-sized four poster bed, freshly made up with crisp linen sheets.

Finn dimmed the lights as Noah led her to the bed, lifting her at the waist so that she sat on the edge of the tall bed, sinking into the lusciously soft comforter. Finn approached and stood behind his brother, his expression somber as he watched Noah kneel to remove Charlotte's stilettos.

Noah traced his fingertips up Charlotte's shins to her knees, moving to take a seat next to her. Finn took a seat on her other side, lacing his fingers with hers. Charlotte looked down at their clasped hands and then up into Finn's luminous, ocean-colored eyes, shuddering with anticipation when Noah's lips touched her shoulder through the thin cotton of her dress, then brushed the exposed skin at her neck.

Finn saw the question in her eyes and gave her a soft smile, cupping her chin with his strong fingers. He lifted her lips as his descended, his mouth seeking hers in a gentle, tentative kiss. Charlotte's lips parted, her tongue darting out to seek Finn's. He was warm and spicy-sweet, his tongue exploring hers with sure strokes, his boldness growing every moment until the kiss turned hot and demanding.

Finn pulled back after a moment and nodded to Noah, drawing her attention to his twin. Charlotte turned to Noah, settling her hands on his shoulders as she sought his mouth. Noah's kiss was more demanding, fiercer than Finn's. Noah's tongue ruled hers in an instant, teasing and flicking and making her moan into his mouth.

Finn's fingers found the zipper at the back of her dress, the cool air against her bare skin giving her goosebumps. Noah's hands came up to tug the sleeves of her dress down and off her arms, his hands coming up to cup her breasts through her lacy pink bra. Finn pushed the dress down, shifting Charlotte a little this way and that to slide her dress all the way off.

Charlotte's fingers found the buttons of Noah's shirt, pulling it from his waist and baring his chest. She sucked in a breath as she looked at him, every inch of bare, tan, muscular perfection. He was lean and strong and hard, his chest smooth under her searching fingers.

She broke from Noah's hungry kiss and turned to Finn, making short work of his tie and shirt, baring him as well. Noah's hands stroked her hips, her ribs, the outer curves of her breasts. Finn pulled the straps of her bra off her shoulders, unhooking the front clasp. Noah pulled the material away and tossed it aside, his hands gripping her waist as he looked over her shoulder, admiring her heavy breasts.

While Noah nuzzled her neck and ear, Finn shaped her breasts, cupping and lifting them. Charlotte gasped as he pinched her nipples, then dropped his head and flicked his hot tongue over one.

"Finn, yes!" Charlotte cried, arching into Noah. Noah's hand slid around to cup and squeeze her free breast, pulling her backward into his lap so that her ass pressed against his long, thick erection, leaving only his pants and her thin panties between.

Charlotte traced the firm muscle of Finn's shoulder, down his chest and over his taut abs, until the found his belt buckle. She unbuttoned and unzipped him, pushing at his pants until he chuckled and pulled back for a moment to shuck them.

Finn was left in nothing but white boxer briefs, the tight fabric clinging to his package and revealing his incredible size. Noah adjusted beneath her, stripping off his own slacks before bringing the backs of her bare thighs down onto his lap once more.

"Lean back, darling," Noah purred in her ear, lifting the thick cascade of her hair with one hand. The tip of his tongue traced the shell of her ear, making her moan. Wet heat trickled low in her body, and her breasts tightened with need even as Finn nuzzled and sucked at her sensitive skin.

Noah leaned back against the bed's pillows, drawing Charlotte back with him. Finn moved her legs so that she lay stretched out on the bed, Noah supporting her and cupping her full breasts. Finn gave her a questioning glance as his fingers tugged at the band of her panties, trailing down to brush her damp mound through the lacy fabric.

"Yes," Charlotte whispered, flushing when Finn stripped off her panties.

"God, you're beautiful..." Finn said, drawing close and kissing her lips once more. He worshipped her shoulders, collarbone, and breast as Noah's fingertips explored her hip, the top of her thigh, her mons...

Finn nudged her knees apart, exposing the damp curls at her bare, heated core. Charlotte cried out when Noah's fingers brushed the top of her slit, now slick with readiness. Two broad fingertips circled her aching clit even as Finn used his teeth on her nipple, giving her quick, gentle bites that made her writhe and moan.

Charlotte lost herself in sensation, her eyes drifting closed as Noah stroked her clit in soft circles. Finn's fingers found her damp core, two thick digits probing her before pressing deep into her taut, wet channel. Charlotte's hips jerked, wetness rushing to her core and covering Finn's fingers.

Noah's hands came up to her hips, adjusting her body once again. Charlotte opened her eyes to find Finn lowering himself to his elbows, dropping a trail of hot kisses from her knee up her inner thigh until his nose brushed her slick lower lips.

"Oh god..." she murmured, bucking her hips against the first touch of his lips against her throbbing clit. Noah tipped her head back, sucking and nipping at her neck before taking her mouth in a consuming kiss.

Finn's lips and tongue licked and swirled around her clit, bringing her to the brink even as Noah's tongue thrust into her mouth, stealing her very breath. Noah's touch on her breasts, the steady pulse of Finn's hot mouth sucking and licking her clit...

Charlotte exploded, darkness and light and every conceivable color bursting within her as she bucked against both her lovers, giving a throaty shout. As her eyes fluttered open once more, her heart pounding in her chest, she gave a feeble chuckle.

"Finn..." she said, tugging him up from the bed. She gave Finn a long, deep kiss, tasting her own essence on his lips and finding it very erotic. Charlotte sucked in a breath, trying to slow her heartbeats, and noticed how badly her whole body was shaking.

Noah nuzzled her ear, his hips gripping her hips.

"Do you want more, Charlotte?" he asked.

"I want you both," she said, hesitant. "But I don't know how... how this works."

Noah's knowing chuckle send a fission of heat down her spine.

"Then both you shall have," he said.

"Why are you two still wearing clothes when I'm completely

naked?" Charlotte teased, Noah and Finn's obvious desire for her making her feel bold.

"We're fools," Finn said, dropping a kiss against her nape as he rose and shucked his boxer briefs. Noah mirrored his movement, and they both chuckled as Charlotte stared at their naked perfection, her eyes widening. Each twin had the thickest, longest, most beautiful cock that Charlotte had ever seen.

Noah glanced a Finn and made a discreet gesture. Finn took Noah's place, sprawling out across the bed with his head resting on a pillow. He took his cock in his hand and gave it a firm stroke, licking his lips as he looked Charlotte up and down.

"Come to me," Finn beckoned. "Straddle me, Charlotte. You were so tight around my fingers, I can't wait to fuck you."

Charlotte gaped for a second, surprised at Finn's dirty mouth, but Noah gave her a light slap on the ass that got her moving. She looked at Noah for a moment, biting her lip.

"Don't worry about me yet, darling," Noah told her. "Let me see you ride his cock."

Charlotte flushed, loving every filthy word that came out of his mouth. She climbed onto the bed, straddling Finn. She ran her fingers up the length of his erection, biting her lip as she thought of the pleasure that awaited her. Never had Charlotte been so dirty, so hungry. Never had she felt so free. Every bit of pleasure only made her want more from both men, and she wanted to experience everything they had to offer.

Finn fisted his cock, lifting and guiding her until the thick crown pressed at her core. Charlotte pressed down, enjoying Finn's tortured groan as her tight channel stretched to accommodate his thickness and length. He filled her so completely, thrusting up into her tightness, making her cry out his name.

Finn set a slow, deep rhythm, rocking up into her body. He gripped her hips to steady her as she began to move, riding him in gentle strokes. She felt Noah's hands brush her back as he knelt behind her, cupping her ass and hips and breasts, encouraging her to move faster.

"Take him deep, Charlotte," Noah purred, his teeth nipping the nape of her neck. Noah's hands pushed her forward, pressing her closer to Finn, who gave her a deep, thrusting kiss to match the movement of his hips. Charlotte lost herself in Finn, his kiss and his cock fueling the fire burning low in her body, heating her blood once more with molten passion.

Noah's hand caressed her lower back, cupped her bare ass. When his fingertips teased the tender crease between her cheeks, she lost her rhythm. She broke her kiss with Finn, who merely turned his face to lick and kiss her neck instead. Their pace slowed as she tried to comprehend Noah's plan.

"Trust me, darling," Noah murmured. A lone fingertip slid down, down, down until it pressed the clenched ring of muscle between her ass cheeks. "I'm going to touch you here, and make you cum."

Noah's touch disappeared for a moment, and he rolled off the bed. When he returned, he used a softly probing fingertip to spread a cool, slick substance over her tight hole.

"Relax for me, Charlotte," Noah urged. "Finn is making you feel so good, making your body burn… Just relax for me. You don't have to move, let Finn do all the work."

Charlotte sought Finn's kiss once more, moaning as he resumed his slow, deep thrusts. She focused on the pleasure, moaning when Noah pressed his fingertip into her body, sliding his finger deep into forbidden territory.

She blushed and cried out when Noah introduced a second finger and slid then both deep, a strange new heat blossoming in her body.

"Good girl," Noah said, using his fingers to mimic the same thrusting rhythm that Finn used to fill her channel. Just as Charlotte began to tighten and truly burn with need, her orgasm nearing, Noah withdrew and spread more cool cream over her ass.

"I'm going to take you, Charlotte," Noah told her. "You're going to cum harder than you ever have in your life, I promise you."

Charlotte looked at Finn, her heart thrumming in her chest. Finn kissed her and gave her a slight nod, and she nodded back. Finn slowed his movements, nearly stopping as he held Charlotte's hips still for Noah. Finn slid his hand between their bodies, his fingers fluttering over Charlotte's clit, making her bite her lip to hold in the scream building in her throat.

Noah's thighs brushed Charlotte's bare ass for a moment, and then she felt the blunt head of his cock at her rear entrance. Finn thrust up into her body in lazy strokes, but Charlotte was riveted on the hot press of Noah's cock into her ass. Noah moved in slow inches, gripping her hips and hissing as he stretched her oversensitive flesh.

Finn pinched her clit, making her cry out, and Noah plunged deep at the same time.

"Fuck, you're so tight. I can't..." Noah cursed, his words trailing off. Heart pounding, body burning, clit pulsing, Charlotte still would have given anything to see Noah's face at that moment.

She lifted her hips, pressing back against Noah, appreciating the stinging pleasure of being so... full. Finn grunted, his breathing labored. Noah set the pace, thrusting and withdrawing, guiding Charlotte's movements as she rode Finn's cock.

Charlotte cried out, her body filled with the two men, starving for release.

"Noah... Finn... Please..." she whimpered.

They moved as one, thrusting hard and fast, Finn's fingers never leaving Charlotte's clit. For a long moment she was suspended in time, sensation and sound rippling through her body, she a mere conduit of their pleasure.

Her peak came in an instant, blowing all thought and choice and knowledge from her mind. Her body clamped down, tight muscles fluttering around the two cocks that penetrated her. The heat and light and colors in her mind had no beginning or end, a vast stretch of pure, mindless, burning satisfaction.

The only thing that drew her down was Noah's growl in her ear and Finn's answering shout, both men stiffening for a split second before pounding into her body without rhythm, each man pulsing hot, salty lashes of seed deep into her body. Charlotte's whole body shook as both men took her primally, reducing her burning need to ashes, shaking her to the very core of her being.

Noah withdrew and collapsed on the bed beside his twin. After a long moment of breathless, silent communication between the two men, Noah sneered at Finn and let out a deep, near-threatening growl. Charlotte tensed, not understanding the sudden aggression, but Noah was already pulling her into his arms, away from his twin.

Noah wrapped his arms around her and laid her out over his own body, taking her lips in a searching, scorching kiss. He stroked her hair, sweeping the tumbled mass from her sweat-slicked back so that he could rub circles over her back, up and down, soothing and cherishing her.

"Noah..." Charlotte whispered, her breath slowing and deepening.

"Shhh, darling," Noah said, kissing the top of her head. He continued to caress her bare back, even after he drew a thin blanket over them both.

Charlotte felt the mattress shift, and a part of her knew that sweet Finn was fleeing the bed. But she was so tired, and Noah's touch felt so good...

Her eyes closed, despite every effort, and darkness soon claimed her overtaxed mind and body.

TEN

Noah floated up from the drowsing sleep he'd found, Charlotte's warm form still wrapped in his arms. He turned his head, seeking his twin, and saw that he'd stepped out onto the hotel room's narrow concrete balcony.

Easing Charlotte from his arms and settling her into the thick comforter, Noah rose and donned his boxer briefs. Stepping out onto the balcony, he saw that Finn had put on his slacks and was buttoning up his shirt. Finn stared out over the St. Louis skyline, gentle rays of sun beginning to light it from the easternmost point on the horizon.

Finn didn't look over at Noah, but his clenched jaw and tense movements made his discontent evident enough.

"What?" Noah asked, folding his arms across his chest and leaning against the metal balcony railing.

"I didn't say anything," Finn said, avoiding Noah's gaze. He continued to dress, tucking his shirt in and rubbing a hand through his close-cropped hair.

"Bad hangover?" Noah asked, trying to make conversation, warm Finn up a little. Finn scowled and started putting on his shoes, bending to tie the laces.

"Alright, seriously. What's your deal?" Noah demanded.

"Nothing," Finn insisted, straightening and leveling Noah with a stony look.

"Bullshit. I can *feel* your lie, Finny. Why are you being such an asshole?" Noah asked.

Finn crossed his arms and leaned against the opposite wall, turning his head to look out at the skyline once more.

"It's just typical, that's all. Who can resist Noah Beran? Not Charlotte, obviously."

Noah growled at his twin.

"You can't be serious right now with this jealous bullshit. She didn't choose me, she chose both of us! We both got a taste, and I don't recall you complaining when you were balls-deep inside her."

"Nothing has changed since last night. I saw the way Charlotte looked at you, all starry-eyed. I heard you calling her 'darling'. We both know how this is going to go down," Finn said. "She's probably half in love with you already. Prince Charming, showing up at the stroke of midnight to win the damsel's heart. It's clear as day who she prefers."

"You've decided that, have you?" Noah challenged.

"I didn't decide anything. I never had a chance," Finn hissed.

"This is not high school, Finn. Charlotte isn't Rebecca Hastings," Noah said, bringing up the first girl they'd ever fought over.

Finn flinched, and Noah was surprised to see that his twin was still sensitive about something that had happened between them over a decade earlier. When he remained silent, Noah pushed on.

"You're a grown-ass man, Finn. You want something, you take it. If it's difficult, you fight for it. Everyone else around you is making choices, moving on, enjoying life. You're the only one who's just… treading water," Noah spat.

"As if this is what I want!" Finn exclaimed. "Do you think I want to be the one who stayed close to home? Do you think I want to be the momma's boy of the family?"

Noah laughed.

"First of all, that's Gavin. Second of all, these are your choices! If you don't like your life, change it!"

"Easy for you to say. You always set goals and go after them, regardless of the rest of us. When Pa got sick, it was just me and Gavin and Ma taking care of him. The rest of you were off living your dreams while I was juggling hospital stays and chemotherapy schedules and…"

Finn broke off with a frustrated huff. He glanced up at Noah, recrimination blazing in his eyes.

"I got into four top-tier PH.d programs. Did you know that? Cornell, Yale, Stanford, NYU. Free rides at all of them."

Noah blinked, confused.

"You did?"

"Yeah, I did. I was planning to get a doctorate so that I could teach at the college level," Finn said, looking more irate than ever.

"I had no idea," Noah admitted.

"Yeah, well, I worked my ass off. My undergrad thesis was published, something that no one in the family deigned to notice. Not that it mattered, because before I could choose a school, Pa got his diagnosis. What was I supposed to do, tell Ma and Gavin that I was too busy shooting for the stars to help them out?" Finn gave a disgusted grunt.

"Pa's been in remission for over a year, Finn. There's nothing holding you back now, is there?" Noah argued, making a sweeping gesture.

"There's always new fires to put out," Finn said, a determined glint in his eyes.

"And you'll just keep running around, doing everything for the Beran clan. Yet somehow, for all that effort, you aren't even in the running to take Pa's place as Alpha. Neither is Gavin," Noah huffed.

From the icy expression on Finn's face, Noah knew he'd found a sore spot.

"Well, this has all been great," Finn said, shaking his head. "Really, such great quality time with my other half."

"You're the one who always instigated these weird threesomes," Noah said with a shrug. "You were sated enough a couple of hours ago."

"Yeah, well now I'm not. You say it's time that I raise my expectations; I guess right now is a great time to start."

With that, Finn brushed past Noah and went back into the hotel room. He stopped and dropped a kiss on Charlotte's head. She shifted and sighed, but didn't wake. Finn stalked out of the suite without a backward glance, leaving Noah alone with a beautiful, curvy blonde and a mind full of dark thoughts.

ELEVEN

Charlotte paced her living room, cell phone in hand, trying to get up the nerve to make a simple phone call. She thumbed through her contact list, hovering over *Noah Beran*.

"Quit being a wimp," she scolded herself. "He's just a guy. This isn't a big deal. Call him and ask him for another date."

Of course, Noah wasn't really just a guy, was he? Charlotte's stomach fluttered as she thought of their last date, at the intense sexual experience she'd shared with Noah and Finn. When she awoke in Noah's arms, Finn nowhere to be found, her confusion quickly gave way to a soul-deep blush at what they'd done only hours before. What she'd encouraged Noah and Finn to do to her body. The wanton way she'd climaxed, harder and longer and better than anything she'd ever experienced before.

When Noah woke, his scrutiny was more than Charlotte could handle. His hand brushed her hip, setting her aflame all over again, and she panicked. Turning down his offer of a leisurely breakfast in bed, with the implication of more soul-rending sex to follow, she dressed and fled. Noah barely had time to put his number in her phone before she was out the door, mentally lashing herself for her complete awkwardness.

Three days later, she'd had enough of driving herself crazy with doubt and recrimination. Charlotte was curious about Noah, couldn't get him out of her mind. The feel of his hands on her skin seemed to be burned into her consciousness. It was different than she'd ever felt about another man, more... grave, somehow.

Taking a deep breath, she hit dial. Noah picked up on the third ring.

"Charlotte?" he asked, his voice a deep rumble. Charlotte shivered and nodded, blushing when she realized that he couldn't see her gesture.

"Hi, Noah," she sighed.

"I was wondering when you were going to call. I've run through most of the interesting tourist attractions in St. Louis," he joked.

"You're still here?" she asked, her heart squeezing.

"Of course. I don't think things are settled between us, do you?"

Charlotte paused for a moment, surprised.

"No, I would say not," she said at last.

"I hope you're calling because you want to see me," Noah said.

"I am," Charlotte said. "I thought you might go out with me tonight, if you're free."

"Completely. What should we do?" Noah asked.

"There's an Italian place I love downtown, I thought we could go there. Or we could see a show at the Fox Theatre," she suggested.

"Dinner sounds good. I'd like us to be able to talk, get to know each other a little more," Noah said. "You know, dazzle you with my personality."

Charlotte couldn't suppress a giggle.

"Alright," she agreed. "I'll text you the address. How does seven o'clock sound?"

"Not as good as right this second, but I'll take what I can get."

Charlotte laughed again before saying goodbye and hanging up. Holding her phone to her chest, she bit her lip to hold back a squeal of excitement. She had another date with Noah Beran!

TWELVE

*C*harlotte sat across the table from Noah, trying to be sneaky about checking him out as he perused the menu. In the candlelight, she noticed that his dark hair had some subtle caramel tints, natural highlights that any brunette woman would kill for. Those caramel tints flirted with the smooth, natural tan of his skin; Charlotte blushed when she realized she knew that Noah's tan was natural, because she'd seen him buck-naked and noticed that he bore no tan lines.

After several moments, Charlotte realized that Noah's searing green-blue gaze was on her face, his lips quirked upward in amusement.

"Interesting thoughts?" he asked, and Charlotte's blush deepened.

Her phone buzzed on the table, and she frowned at it. She grabbed the phone and stuck it in her bag.

"Sorry. Um, no. Nothing interesting at all," she lied, opening her menu and pretending deep interest in the long list of pastas and entrees.

"Should we order some wine?" Noah asked.

Charlotte made a face.

"I overdid it on Saturday. The idea of wine turns my stomach," she admitted. "I think I drank more than a bottle by myself."

Noah gave her a sage nod.

"How about calamari? Are you an appetizer person?" he asked. The expression on his face made it pretty clear that an affirmative answer was the only correct one. Before she could answer, Charlotte phone buzzed again.

"I'm sorry. It'll stop in a second. I don't know who'd be calling right now, except..." She stopped, biting her lip. *Except work.* It could easily be the hospital calling her with vital information about one of her patients, though she didn't work again until the following evening.

"Charlotte." Noah reached out and pulled her menu flat against the table, then covered her hand with the warmth of his own. "Just take the call. It's not a big deal."

After another moment of guilty debate, Charlotte nodded. She grabbed her phone and checked her texts, her stomach sinking in an instant.

"The face you're making doesn't bode well for our evening," Noah commented. Charlotte looked up at him, guilt expanding in her chest even as she struggled to stay calm.

"It's work. One of my longterm patients isn't doing well. She might not make it through the night," she sighed.

"All right, then," Noah said, rising to his feet.

"I'm so sorry, I wouldn't have made our date for tonight—" Charlotte began.

"Don't even start apologizing. Let's go," Noah said.

"We can reschedule," Charlotte said.

"Let's just get you over to the hospital, okay?" Noah asked.

"Oh..." Charlotte paused, taken aback. "I was just going to take the train."

Noah gave her a long look, pursing his lips.

"I don't think so," he said. He pulled out his wallet and tossed a twenty on the table, though they hadn't been served anything more than water yet. "My car's in the valet. Let's get your coat, darling."

Charlotte followed him, unable to stop the shiver that skated across her skin at his casual use of the endearment. Noah took over, getting her coat and the car in no time, and before she knew it he was pulling into a space outside the hospital.

When Noah climbed out of the car and came around to open her door, Charlotte felt even guiltier. Not only was he being more than calm about their blown date, he was being a complete gentleman. Then, somehow, Noah managed to take things even further.

"I'm going up with you. I'll stay out of the way, I promise," he said, giving her a soft smile.

"Oh, Noah... I could be here all night," Charlotte said, shaking her head.

"I've got tons of books on my phone. I'll make friends with the nurses," he said, taking her arm and escorting her into the hospital's wide glass automatic doors. "Don't worry about me, okay?"

Charlotte took a deep breath and plunged ahead, leading him to the employee elevators and up to her wing. The second that she hit her ward, every single nurse was staring at them. More precisely, at the incredibly hot man on her arm.

Connie, her closest nurse friend, cocked an eyebrow. Connie eyed Charlotte's sage green dress and white heels, Noah's slick dark blue suit and tie, and then her own pink rubber-ducky-covered scrubs.

"You brought a guest?" Connie asked, her chocolate-brown eyes devouring Noah inch by inch, head to toe.

"Yeah... We were sort of... interrupted," Charlotte sighed. She made the quick introductions. "Connie, this is my friend Noah. Noah, this is Connie. She can get you settled somewhere comfortable, get you something to drink if you want."

Charlotte gave Connie a pleading look, swallowing when Connie flashed her a mischievous smile in return.

"I'll take good care of your man, I promise," Connie said.

"Okay. I'm going to grab a gown and a mask and go see Sarah," Charlotte said, referring to her seven-year-old patient with acute myelogenous leukemia.

Connie's smile dimmed, her eyes softening. She nodded and patted Charlotte's shoulder, turning to lead Noah to the waiting room. Charlotte headed down the hallway, glancing back once to find Noah's gaze on her, his expression pensive and concerned. Stomach churning, she forced herself to turn away and focus on her patient. In Charlotte's book, her patients would always come before the men in her life, no matter how sexy and wonderful they might be.

THIRTEEN

Bleary-eyed and emotionally exhausted, Charlotte stripped off her gown and mask and tossed them into the trash near the nurses' station. She'd long since traded her heels for a pair of practical flats from her work locker, a backup pair that she frequently made use of on middle-of-the-night trips just such as this one.

She checked her phone, sighing when she saw that it was nearly four in the morning. She'd missed half a dozen texts from Abby, asking how her second date went. Charlotte huffed out a tired breath and gathered up her stuff. Feeling like a zombie, she headed for the elevators. When a pair of big hands landed on her waist, she actually shrieked and jumped.

It was Noah, looking rumpled yet somehow still delicious.

"You— you're still here," Charlotte croaked. Seeing him crumpled the last tiny bit of her reserve, and tears pooled in her eyes. She hadn't cried the whole night until she looked up into those sea-green eyes, saw her own sadness reflected there.

"Hey, hey," Noah said, his voice soft. He turned her around and looked down into her face, his eyes searching her face. "Are you okay?"

"No," Charlotte said, sagging. When Noah pulled her close and wrapped his arms around her, holding her up as much as he was embracing her. He was so big and warm and firm, felt so good in her moment of complete weakness. They stayed like that for a couple of minutes, Charlotte holding back tears as she let Noah comfort her.

"Let's get you home," Noah suggested, brushing a stray lock of hair from her face. Charlotte could only imagine that she looked like a complete wreck.

"Actually…" Charlotte said, shaking her head. "I have a thing I do. A ritual, I guess."

Noah's brow arched, but he just waited patiently for her explanation.

"When I lose a patient, I go to this diner and have a last meal in their honor. It sounds dumb, but it's sort of…" Charlotte trailed off with a shrug.

"Closure," Noah supplied.

Charlotte tipped her chin up to look at him. Noah joked a lot, and he was wildly sexy, but there was something more there, lurking under the surface. Something dark, a part of him that understood pain and death. Thinking of his big family and seeming air of privilege, she wondered how he'd acquired such depth.

"Right," she said finally. "Closure."

"Hope this diner has omelets," Noah said, giving her another of those smiles. That deadly dimple flashed in his cheek, and in her frail state she thought her heart might just give out right then and there.

"You really don't have to come," she said.

"We're not even having this conversation. Come on," Noah said, taking her hand as he pressed the button to call the elevator. "I'm *starving*."

For the second time that night, Charlotte let Noah take the lead, even though none of their activities benefited him in the least. As they drove to the diner in silence, Charlotte realized that she had some serious revising to do where her impression of Noah's character was concerned.

FOURTEEN

Noah settled into the cramped diner booth across from Charlotte, feeling a little shell-shocked. He'd seen several facets of her before: the dutiful Berserker woman, the social flirt, the protective cousin. The pleasure-hungry conquest, something he would certainly never forget.

But this side of Charlotte, this deeply compassionate creature... this was something he could barely wrap his head around. Her eyes were red-rimmed, her cheeks flushed pink from crying, her hair thrown up into a messy ponytail. She'd changed shoes at some point, making her noticeably shorter than he was used to. And yet, she was more beautiful than ever.

Noah realized that Charlotte was blushing under his appraising gaze. Snapping up a menu, he peered at the limited list of choices in order to distract himself. After ordering a veritable mountain of food for himself plus pancakes and coffee for Charlotte, he found himself at a loss for words. His normal M.O. was levity, which didn't work at all in light of Charlotte's rough night. Luckily, she saved him.

"So how many bad magazines did you read while I was working?" Charlotte asked.

Noah grinned, glad that she was making things so easy for him.

"I only got through about three, actually. Connie introduced me to one of your patients and we hung out for a long time."

Charlotte's brows shot up in surprise, and Noah felt himself nearly insulted by her reaction.

"Who?" she asked, brow puckering.

"Max. He was awesome," Noah said, keeping his tone casual. Truly, the young panther shifter had started things off with a surly-ass attitude. But things had turned around quickly when Noah spotted the kid's Xbox.

"He talked to you?" Charlotte asked, her look turning skeptical.

"Yeah. We played Metal Gear Solid for like... four hours. He said he has trouble sleeping."

Charlotte nodded slowly.

"Yeah. He's a typical preteen boy, keeping it all inside, but he's really sick."

"Is it— would it be rude for me to ask what's wrong with him?" Noah asked.

"He has osteosarcoma, bone cancer. It's super painful," Charlotte said, looking down as she toyed with her coffee mug.

"Where are his people?" Noah asked. When Charlotte's expression went black, he wondered if he'd overstepped somehow.

"Max is in the foster care system. He's been in and out of Children's Hospital for years now, and he's never had the same foster parent more than a couple of times. No one wants the burden of a kid who's that sick."

Noah frowned.

"What about the local cat shifters? Shouldn't they take him in?" he asked.

"There aren't any panther packs in this part of the country, and the lions seem unconcerned. Believe me, I've tried."

"Well..." Noah tried to find the right words, then shook his head. "That fucking blows."

Charlotte nodded and sipped her coffee.

"So you guys got along, huh?" she asked. There was some

emotion brimming in her eyes, something that Noah couldn't begin to read.

"Yep. I told him I'd come back this week."

Charlotte downright scowled, her sudden intensity making the hairs on Noah's neck raise.

"You shouldn't make promises to him. Kids like Max seem tough, but they're really lonely."

Noah raised his hands, feeling defensive.

"I just said I'd come back this week, and I will," he said.

"I'm not—" Charlotte stopped, and sighed. "Just don't promise him anything else, okay? He's had it so rough. He needs stability."

And not globe-trotting Noah Beran, seemed to be left unsaid. Charlotte was starting to sound an awful lot like Finn.

The waitress delivered their food and they dug in. Noah hadn't realized how hungry he was until he'd plowed through a mountain of bacon and French toast, plus an omelet.

"This place is incredible," he said when he'd finished, stacking his empty plates at the edge of the table. "I've eaten at a lot of diners, and this one is in my top five. Easy."

Charlotte chuckled.

"I'm so glad I could impress you," she teased.

"Well. It's no breakfast in Paris, but it's pretty damned satisfying."

"I eat here a lot. Not just after... you know, a patient passes away. It's comfort food, for sure," she said. "Though I'm not usually such a wreck. Sarah was with us for almost a year. I thought she was going to turn the corner and go into remission."

There was a long pause in the conversation while Noah tried to figure out the right thing to say. Charlotte's face reddened, and she gave him a guilty glance.

"I'm sorry. I know this isn't good conversation. This is like, the worst second date ever."

Noah reached across the table and took her hand.

"I'm not uncomfortable with death," he said, keeping his sentiment simple.

"No?" Charlotte asked, cocking her head.

"No, not really. Everyone teases me about my job and how I just get to travel and hang, but I actually see a lot of terrible shit. Suicide bombers, police assaults on college kids, women and children killed by American drone strikes..." He waved a hand. "And me, right in the middle."

Charlotte shuddered.

"I can't see why you'd want to do that," she said.

"There's a reason why journalists cover war zones and political uprisings, you know. It's not just sensationalism. When journalists and photographers do stories on the people effected by violence, they bring the issues to the Western world. A lot of the aid money and peacekeeping troops and medical support that these countries need comes from the West, but it doesn't come unless politicians make it happen. If citizens don't see the stories and realize that people are in trouble, the politicians aren't interested. Journalists are just one little cog in the whole grand scheme," Noah explained.

"I had no idea," Charlotte said, looking impressed. "It seems like you're really passionate about it."

Noah shrugged.

"It's started to wear me down. First I was lonely overseas, and then jaded. Now I see these amazing things, terrible things, and I just feel sort of... empty."

Noah swallowed and reached for his coffee cup, realizing that he'd said a bit more than he intended.

"Maybe you just need to be a little more grounded. How often do you go home to see your family?"

"Not very often. I have all these great childhood memories, and they're the best ones I've got. I don't want them to get the wear and tear of everyday life, you know?"

Charlotte considered him for a long moment.

"You're lucky, you know. My family isn't nearly as stable."

"I'd expect it to be pretty quiet if you're not in the Alpha's family," Noah replied.

"That's the thing. My father was Alpha for over a decade, until my teens."

"He stepped down? Was he sick or something?"

"No, my uncle Jared actually challenged him. Uncle Jared won trial by combat, and graciously *deigned* to let my father keep his life." There was no missing the sarcasm in her tone as she spoke of the event.

"How old were you?" Noah asked. Losing Alpha status must have crushed her father, and brought a great deal of confusion and embarrassment to Charlotte.

"Fourteen. My parents have always pressured me to stand out, be this irresistible girl that no one can turn down. My father wants me to take an Alpha as a mate, someone who will lead a clan one day. I think he feels like he'll have power and influence again. Which is funny considering that I go home about as much as you do."

"I think you're irresistible, darling," Noah informed her. "I'll never be a major Alpha, though. Too much politicking."

Charlotte gave him an amused glance.

"That doesn't matter to me a bit. And all joking aside, you really need to see your family. If you can tolerate being in a room with them, you should do it as much as possible. You're much more lucky than you know."

Noah ducked his head, acknowledging her words. The waitress brought the bill, and Noah stared Charlotte down when she tried to give the waitress her credit card. He handed the waitress a wad of cash and then ushered Charlotte out of the restaurant.

FIFTEEN

Noah drove Charlotte home, following her directions to a cute blue bungalow complete with a picket fence. He got out and opened her door, helping her out of the car and ushering her up the walkway to the house. He paused at the front door as she fished out her keys, thinking he shouldn't invite himself in, but Charlotte merely glanced up at him with a tired smile. She unlocked the door and grabbed his hand, tugging him along in her wake. Noah certainly wasn't going to resist; he was curious about her life, and wanted to see her living space.

"Your house is beautiful," he told her, looking around at her neat, comfortable open living room and kitchen.

"Thanks," Charlotte sighed. She went to the kitchen and opened the fridge pulling out two bottles of water and offering him one before dropping onto the oversized tan leather couch. Noah took a long sip of his, still standing as he looked around. She had several bookshelves, all overflowing with texts of every kind. A large TV and DVD collection, a Macbook sitting on the coffee table, and even a pretty nice sound system.

"Come sit with me?" Charlotte asked, turning her sapphire gaze up to him. She looked a lost and tired, in need of more comfort than diner food could give.

Noah's lips quirked as he abandoned the bottle of water on

the coffee table, sitting down and pulling Charlotte close. He wrapped her in his arms, intending only to hold her, though his body hardened at the simple contact.

"You smell so good," Charlotte murmured, her face pressed against his chest. Before Noah could blink, Charlotte shifted and pressed her lips to his, her arms twining around his neck. Her kiss was hard and hungry, her need evident as her lips parted, tongue seeking his.

Noah groaned as his arm tightened around her waist, crushing Charlotte's incredible curves against his body. Her breasts pressed against his chest, making him yearn to cup and lick and squeeze them even as he deepened the kiss.

Charlotte took control, her hands plucking at the buttons on his shirt. Noah sucked at her earlobe, nipped the sensitive flesh at her neck, traced her collarbone with his tongue. Charlotte's chest heaved, her breath coming in short pants. She kicked off her shoes and shifted on the couch, adjusting her dress.

Noah growled low in his throat when she wriggled out of her panties, straddling his lap.

"I need you, Noah," she whispered, her fingers working at his belt and zipper. She shoved his pants partway down his hips, making him hiss with pleasure when her fingers wrapped around his aching cock. She pumped her fist up and down his length, and Noah ground into her, giving her control. She stripped off his shirt, dropping kisses to his neck and shoulders, her luscious mouth burning his too-warm skin.

Noah pushed down the shoulders of her dress and the straps of her bra, roughly shoving it to her waist to bare her glorious, full breasts. As he cupped and nuzzled the soft globes, Charlotte moaned and pulled up the hem of her dress, her hand guiding his erection to her hot, slick core.

Noah couldn't hold back a rumbling growl as he slid into Charlotte's tight channel, thrusting deep.

"Yes!" Charlotte cried, her hands running up his bare chest to brace on his shoulders.

Noah gripped her hips, setting an insistent, driving rhythm as he guided her movements, thrusting up into her willing flesh.

Charlotte tightened around him immediately, and he knew she wouldn't last long. He was floored, his body tensing, balls drawing tight with the need to finish.

Charlotte's nails raked his shoulders, marking his skin, a low keening sound escaping her throat. She shattered, her body pulsing around his cock, triggering his own release. Noah lost his breath as he spasmed, grinding up into her, jetting his release into her body in long pumps.

When at last he slowed, pulling Charlotte into his arms and down onto his sweat-dampened chest, she gave a satisfied sigh that stoked his male ego like nothing else possibly could. She was so soft and sweet, lying sated in his embrace.

She lifted her chin to give him a final, drugging kiss before climbing off his lap with a chuckle.

"That was not what I came in here for," Noah informed her.

"No?" Charlotte asked, arching a brow.

"I meant to be comforting," he said, his lips lifting at the corners.

"I feel very comfortable right now," she said.

"You should always feel comfortable," he said, leaning in to brush a lock of hair that fell across her forehead at a haphazard angle. "You're incredible, and you deserve that much."

Charlotte gave him a bemused look, catching his hand and lacing her fingers with his. Her thumb rubbed lazy circles on his palm, the sensation making his heart tighten uncomfortably.

"Uh huh," was her only reply.

"You don't think so? You're enough to make Finn and me both crazy. I staked a claim on you, and now he's barely speaking to me."

Charlotte stiffened, her hand slipping from his grasp.

"You're fighting because of me?" she asked, her expression hardening.

"Well, there are other elements. But right now, you're the main event."

"Noah…" she said, her tone growing sharp. "I think you're incredible, too, but I won't be the reason you're at odds with your brother."

"Charlotte, don't worry about what's between me and Finn. It's complicated," Noah warned.

"I don't want to be a problem. I won't be," she insisted.

"That's—" Noah gave a huff of frustration. "That's not how family works, Charlotte. It's personal, and more involved than you can know."

Charlotte's eyebrows shot up, her offense evident.

"I don't understand how families work? Jesus, Noah. You are so ungrateful. You know, maybe you don't understand how relationships work, period."

Charlotte shot to her feet, Noah rising with a scowl.

"Are you serious right now?" he asked.

"I think you should leave," she declared, her chin lifting. The dominant bear in him saw her defenses coming up, told him that he shouldn't push her any harder right now.

"Fine," he said. He didn't miss the flash of disappointment on her face, but he didn't know how to talk Charlotte down from the impasse, either.

Too soon, Noah found himself making a quiet, angry walk out to his car. He glanced back at Charlotte's house, seeing little movement in the curtains at the front window. When stillness reigned for another half minute, he growled and got into his car, not believing how the evening had ended.

SIXTEEN

Finn Beran frowned as he packed his suitcase, meticulously folding and rolling each item, the monotonous activity soothing his mind. After almost a week of sightseeing and awkward social introductions via the Krall clan, he was ready to return home. He had one final event early in the evening, a date he'd half-heartedly accepted at the last minute, but after that he was catching the red-eye back to Montana. Fall break was almost up, and Finn was required to attend a teachers' workshop the day before classes recommenced.

A knock on the hotel room door made him pause; there were only a few people who might be knocking, and he didn't especially want to talk to any of them. When Finn swung the door open, he wasn't terribly surprised to find Noah standing there.

His twin raised his hands, a conciliatory gesture.

"I just want to talk," Noah said.

Finn stared Noah down for a long moment, debating with himself. When he stepped back from the door, Noah came in and dropped into a seat by the window, seeming ill at ease. Noah cast a glance the clothes and open suitcase spread out over the king-sized bed, his lips pressing into a grim line.

"I'd think a man who's gotten the woman he wanted would look a little more cheerful," Finn said, returning to his packing.

"I'm sorry for what I said."

Finn looked up at his twin, surprised at the non sequitur.

"Okay..." Finn said, giving him a shrug. He never stayed mad at Noah for long, but that didn't mean his feelings weren't hurt.

"I mean it, Finny." Noah's green gaze seared into Finn's, and he stilled his hands to listen. "I shouldn't have said any of that. I do think you deserve more, but you've sacrificed a lot for the family. I didn't know the extent of it."

Finn swallowed, his lips turning down into a deep frown.

"It's in the past," Finn said.

"No, it isn't. Just because Pa is feeling better... Nothing has changed for you, and it's not fair," Noah told him.

"There's nothing to be done," Finn sighed. "Life goes on. School's starting up again in a few days. That's just how it is."

"You're not going back to teaching," Noah told him. Finn squared off at his brother, his temper rising.

"What are you talking about?"

"I've already got you another interview at Cornell and Stanford. I'm going to reach out to our brothers, use family connections to get you PH.d interviews at all the top programs in the country. Anywhere you want to go."

Finn rolled his eyes.

"It's not that simple. Even if I can get in after taking so much time off, I couldn't afford to do it now. I have a mortgage, and..." he trailed off, growing frustrated.

"You'll sell your place, because you're going to move anyway. And as for the rest of the money, Cameron and I are going to bankroll you for as long as you need. We've already worked all the details out."

Finn gaped at his brother, completely taken aback.

"You— what?" he asked, baffled. Noah raised a dark brow, a trace of amusement on his lips.

"I don't want hear it," Noah insisted. "It's all decided, as long as you have the guts to take what you want. And you do. You're my brother, every bit as strong as me. I know you like I know myself, and I know that this is what you need. So... reach out and take it."

"Why are you doing this all the sudden?" Finn asked,

perplexed. "You all but left the family years ago, and now you're playing the doting twin?"

Pain flashed in Noah's expression, and he gave a slow nod.

"I haven't been half the brother or son I should have been. For that, I'm sorry. I just got so wrapped up in my job, in the lives of my subjects… I wasn't even taking care of myself, much less thinking about my future and my family at home."

Finn came around the bed and sat down across from his brother, reaching out to take his hand, giving it a brief squeeze before releasing him. He could see Noah's internal struggle, his exhaustion and unhappiness and a dozen other things that made Finn's heart lurch.

"Noah… It's really okay. I could never stay mad at you. As for the rest of the family, Luke and Cam and Wyatt haven't been around much more than you have. Gavin and I are the exception, sadly."

"At least you have some roots. I quit my job at the Tribune yesterday, and now I've got nothing," Noah sighed.

"You've got Charlotte," Finn suggested.

Noah's expression pinched, a look that Finn knew all too well.

"Oh, shit. What did you do?" Finn asked.

They sat together in Finn's hotel room for hours, talking about their lives until Finn was nearly late for his last St. Louis date. Noah told him about Charlotte, about his time overseas, about everything. Finn's heart grew heavy with the things that Noah had witnessed, but there was no overcoming the relief and pleasure he felt at mending fences with his twin. As Noah poured out his conflicted feelings about the woman they'd shared just days before, the beginnings of a plan flickered to life in Finn's mind.

SEVENTEEN

Checking the address for a third time, Finn hefted his suitcase as he entered a tiny hole-in-the-wall bistro. Scanning the room, he spotted Abby Krall sitting at a table with several other women. Right on time, as she'd promised as they texted back and forth. Though she'd been surprised at first, when Finn explained his plan and his motives, Charlotte's cousin had been more than accommodating. Finn wondered exactly how much arm-twisting Abby had done to get Charlotte here on such short notice and at eleven p.m., too.

Finn looked at his watch, realizing that he needed to get this done soon. His flight was leaving St. Louis in less than two hours, and he still had to head over to the airport after this.

Abby spotted him and gave him a subtle wave, to which Finn nodded in reply. Abby jumped up and leaned over to talk to the woman next to her; Finn couldn't see Charlotte's face but her silhouette was unmistakable.

Charlotte rose, allowing Abby to lead her to the bar. Finn approached, stepping up behind Charlotte as he admired her long blonde hair and soft curves. A small part of him wished that he'd fought for her, that he could lay claim to Charlotte as his mate, but an equal part knew that if she'd been the right woman, he wouldn't have been able to resist.

"Charlotte," he said, keeping his voice low.

Abby took a few steps back when Charlotte whirled, the brunette giving the blonde a shrug that seemed to say, *Sorry, I had to do it.* Charlotte turned to face Finn, her throat working silently as her wide eyes took in his tall frame and his suitcase.

"You're leaving," she said. Though she kept her voice level, her eyes couldn't hide her hurt and anger.

"I am, but I don't think it's going to effect you unduly," Finn said.

Charlotte's lips parted, her eyes darkening with understanding.

"Finn," she breathed. Finn actually chuckled at her relief. As gone as his twin was on Charlotte, she seemed at least as attached to Noah.

"I'm on my way to the airport, so I can't talk long. I just wanted to ask you to give Noah another chance."

Charlotte frowned.

"Why are you here apologizing for him?" she asked.

"Because my brother is stubborn idiot," Finn said, keeping it simple.

Charlotte's expression eased by a hint, but she was by no means pleased.

"He didn't send you, did he?" Charlotte asked.

"No. He told me what happened, and I felt bad for him. He's the smartest person I know, but he has no idea what to do with a woman like you."

Charlotte relaxed another bare inch, canting her head to the side.

"He wasn't very nice to me. I mean, he was, but then he said some things that I found... distasteful," Charlotte said.

"He told me. I think he feels like an asshole, but he doesn't know how to approach you." Finn paused. "Listen, I can't speak for him. I can't tell you what to do. I just want to tell you that my brother is an honorable guy, underneath all the bullshit. I know he cares for you, and I hope you two will keep seeing one another. That's all."

Charlotte pursed her lips, and gave Finn a slow nod.

"I like Noah, too. I'm sure you've realized that already. I just need to take a few days to think things over. I want to make a good decision," Charlotte said.

Finn gave her a soft smile.

"I'm sure you will. See you around, Charlotte."

With that, Finn picked up his suitcase and headed back outside. He hailed a cab and jumped in, headed for the airport. Pulling out his phone, he shot Noah a quick text.

You'd better make this up to Charlotte. I opened the door for you.

Noah didn't respond, but Finn hadn't expected him to. After mulling over his brother's situation for a few more minutes, Finn turned his thoughts forward. It was time that he focused on his own future, went out and did some work for himself.

EIGHTEEN

Charlotte heaved a sigh as she entered the nurses' locker room. Her feet and back ached, her head throbbed, and after work her third twelve-hour shift in a row, she was exhausted. She'd pulled the night shift last night, which meant that she would get home just as all her neighbors were heading to work. That part always threw her even more off kilter, for some reason. Watching people putting their kids in the car, double checking to make sure they had their science projects and lunches, always made Charlotte feel a strange emptiness in the pit of her stomach.

"As if that's not already happening right now," she grumbled.

Charlotte opened her locker and pulled out a pair of flip flops, dropping onto a bench to take off her tennis shoes.

"You okay?" came a voice.

Charlotte nearly jumped out of her skin before turning to find Connie standing behind her, her own tennis shoes in hand.

"Jeez, you scared me," Charlotte said, shaking her head. "You coming on shift?"

"Yep," Connie answered, plopping down beside Charlotte to change her shoes. It was a familiar rhythm for them both, as they'd worked together in this ward for over three years. Nurses came and went in Children's Hospital, but Connie and Charlotte were mainstays in their little section. Not everybody could handle the really tough cases, the ones that ended in tragedy as often as not.

"Charlotte, you look exhausted," Connie said. Charlotte looked up to find her coworker's concerned gaze lingering on her face.

"Yeah, I haven't been sleeping that well. I'm starting to really worry about Max this time," she admitted. "His most recent round of labs really don't look good."

"Shit," Connie muttered under her breath. "And he's been in such a good mood the last few days."

"Yeah. It's a nice change. A little weird, but nice." Charlotte shrugged.

"He doesn't get to hang out with a lot of guys. No father figure in his life. Now your man friend is giving him some attention—"

"WHAT?" Charlotte asked, accidentally flinging one of her tennis shoes across the room.

"Noah," Connie grunted, lacing up her shoes.

"What about Noah, exactly?" Charlotte demanded to know.

"He's been here every day this week." Connie glanced up, giving Charlotte an odd look. "I figured you knew. You're the one who brought him here in the first place."

"I—" Charlotte hesitated. She certainly didn't want to do anything to stop Noah from visiting Max. Especially if it was the reason for Max's recent change in attitude. "It's fine. Noah's great."

Charlotte tried her hardest not to frown as she said the last part. Noah was actually really nice and great. If he'd managed to show up and apologize, she probably would have already forgiven him. A blush crept over her cheeks when she pictured just what that *forgiveness* would entail, if she had her way.

"Maybe you should go get some sleep. Take some melatonin or something," Connie suggested.

"I think a nice hot bath should do it," Charlotte said. *And maybe half a bottle of wine...*

Charlotte told Connie goodbye and rushed home, desperate to have some time alone to relax. In short order she was slipping into a hot bubble bath, moaning aloud when she took her first sip of the Malbec she'd uncorked.

She let her mind drift, her lips quirking as she came back to thoughts of Noah over and over again. Her libido was usually fairly quiet, sated with a couple of solo sessions a month, but now she recognized the only tightness and tension left in her body as desire. She wanted Noah again, couldn't stop thinking of his sleek, muscular body, of how his big frame made her feel small and delicate, of the throaty sounds he'd made as he touched her, fucked her—

Her phone rang. Charlotte's eyes snapped open, her face flushing as she realized that her fingertips were stroking her own nipple.

Busted.

She knelt in the tub, wiping her hand on a towel and leaning away from the water before answering.

"Hello?" she asked.

"Charlotte," Noah replied. His voice made her shiver with anticipation. Was this finally the apology and booty call that she so dearly wanted?

"Hi, Noah," she said. Her voice came out high and breathy, making her feel silly.

"Um… I did something bad," he said.

Charlotte pursed her lips, thinking that it was a weird way to word an apology.

"Listen, Noah—" she started.

"No, no. Um. Hold on for a second. This isn't like, a you and me thing. I did something dumb like an hour ago, and I need your help. I'm in way over my head."

Charlotte was frozen for a moment before the nurse in her kicked into gear.

"Tell me what happened," she sighed.

"Can you… can I come pick you up? I'm already in your part of town." Charlotte had never heard Noah so uncomfortable, and curiosity seized her.

"Okay," she agreed after a beat.

"Dress comfortably. We'll be there in five," he warned before disconnecting the call.

We? Charlotte blinked at her phone for a second before scrambling to get out of the bath and get ready. She managed to get herself into a red dress and white flats, and throw a few of her things in a tote bag. Pausing to look in the mirror, she put on a little mascara and ran her fingers through her long, damp locks.

She heard a car horn honk outside and took a deep breath, readying herself. When she stepped outside, she found Noah sitting in the driver's seat of a convertible, with the top down... and Max was in the passenger seat, waving enthusiastically.

"What in the..." Charlotte's stomach flip-flopped. Noah jumped out of the car and met her halfway across her yard, his expression nervous.

"I... did something," he said, his shoulders hunched. In another situation, his remorse would have been adorable, but right now Charlotte was floored.

"What is Max doing here?" she hissed, stepping close to Noah. She shot a worried glance at Max, who seemed both elated and perfectly healthy. Unfortunately, she knew the latter simply wasn't true.

"He begged me to bring him to the river for a day. He said he wanted to go one last time, and I couldn't say no," Noah said, rubbing a hand over the back of his neck.

"Noah, Max is really, really sick. He can't just go gallivanting around like this!"

"He's dying, Charlotte. He told me so himself."

Charlotte opened her mouth, and then closed it again, glancing at Max.

"He talked to you about his cancer?" she asked.

"Yeah. He's kind of... resigned about it," Noah said, looking uncomfortable. "I asked him if I could do something for him, and I meant like... get him some new Xbox games or a pizza... This is what he asked for."

"And you called me in to do damage control? I could lose my job for this, Noah."

Noah winced, looking chagrined.

"I'm sorry. I just... I can't take him by myself. If something happens... I don't even know CPR or anything. He brought some of his medications, but I have no idea how they work or..."

Noah left off, heaving a sigh. Charlotte looked at him for a long moment, wavering. In the end, Noah reached out and grabbed her wrist, tugging her close. He looked down at her, his green-blue eyes blazing, his eyes bright with emotion.

"Please, Charlotte. No one has to know that you came with us. Max won't say anything. Please."

The humbleness of his words took her breath away. She'd seen several different sides of Noah: the snob, the jester, the seducer, the intellectual, the jerk. But this, this man who looked at her like his whole world depended on her, this was a facet that she couldn't spurn.

"Alright," she said, stiffening when Noah wrapped her in his arms and kissed her. The embrace was over in a heartbeat, and before she knew it Noah was leading her to the car and helping Max into the back seat. Charlotte gulped as she settled in and put on her seat belt, wondering if they were all making a terrible mistake.

NINETEEN

"You are a fool, Charlotte Krall," she scolded herself.

One look at Max's excited expression had toppled Charlotte's qualms about giving him a "day off", as they were now calling it. A stop at Target had provided towels, sunscreen, bottled water, snacks, and a pair of trunks for Max. Charlotte gave Noah directions to her favorite quiet swimming hole, less than an hour outside St. Louis proper. Every kid around here grew up swimming in the river, blissfully ignorant of their state's land-locked status.

The sweet intention behind the day, and Noah's blossoming friendship with Max, had sealed the deal. How could anyone refuse a sick boy or a gorgeous Berserker male?

Now Charlotte held a hand to her brow, shielding her eyes from the late afternoon sun as she stared down the beach, waiting. When she finally spotted an enormous bear and a small panther padding back toward her, she released a long sigh. She'd begged Max not to shift, fearing that he'd use too much of his precious energy, but he'd taken off anyway. Thank goodness Noah had been a good sport, shifting and following Charlotte's patient. They'd been gone a long time now, and Charlotte had begun to worry that something was terribly wrong.

When Noah and Max finally made it back to the blanket,

shifting and shaking sand from their bodies as they reached from their clothes, Charlotte let herself relax a little.

"Okay. I think that's enough for today, don't you?" Charlotte asked, handing Max the pile of clothes sitting beside their messy spread of beach towels.

Max sprawled on one end of their blanket pallet, leaving Charlotte and Noah in close quarters on the other end. They'd played in the water, napped, and had a nice late lunch around four. Charlotte kept looking at the time, knowing that she needed to wrap this up and get Max back to his hospital bed. His vibrancy was quickly fading now, though he was doing his best to hide it.

"I'm going in the water one more time," Max told them.

"Okay. We have to start packing up here soon, buddy," Noah told Max. Charlotte arched a brow, impressed. She'd assumed that she was going to be here to lay down the law and act as Max's nanny, but Noah had taken charge completely. On another day, this might have just been a relaxing day. *If only*, Charlotte kept thinking.

Max ran off and dove into the water, making Charlotte wince with nerves. He surfaced and splashed around, making a big deal of being energetic and happy.

Charlotte gave Noah a knowing look, and he nodded back to her.

"I hate to have to make him leave, but I think he's going conk out pretty soon," Noah said.

"Yep. There is absolutely no doubt about it," Charlotte agreed.

"Thank you for coming with us," Noah said, snagging her hand in his big one.

"I didn't have a hell of a lot of choice in the matter," Charlotte said with a roll of her eyes.

"Yeah. Sorry about that," Noah said. He really did seem contrite, which mollified Charlotte's anger. Her initial shock and ire had faded as the hours passed. It was impossible to be upset when Max was so happy and Noah was being so sweet and gentlemanly.

Charlotte scooted a little closer to Noah, unable to resist the lure of his warmth and strength. She looked up at him, startled all over again by the handsomeness of his facial features, the taut muscles evidenced beneath his gray flannel shirt and dark jeans. He even wore Converse sneakers, making him look like nothing so much as the to-die-for lead singer of some hot rock band.

Charlotte reached up and brushed his hair back from his forehead, running her thumb along the stubble-laced line of his jaw. She sucked in a soft breath and pressed her lips to his, trying her hardest to keep things light, trying to remember that Max was only twenty yards away.

Noah caught her lower lip between his teeth, giving it a gentle nip, and Charlotte had to hold in a moan of desire. Were they alone, they would unquestionably be halfway nude and doing something much, much less innocent than a little kissing.

Noah pulled back and looked at her.

"I'm sorry for what I said the other night, about family. I was just spouting off," he said.

Charlotte nodded.

"It's okay. I mean, not what you said. But people say things, it happens. I should have reacted better."

"I guess at least we already got our first fight out of the way," Noah said, giving her a full, dazzling smile. He had the most gorgeous smile, his perfect teeth and lips lighting up his whole face, laugh lines softening his Alpha demeanor.

"First fight, huh?" Charlotte said, giving him a smirk.

"Right. I haven't had a lot of serious relationships, but I hear that the first fight is an important rite of passage," Noah intoned.

Before Charlotte could respond, Max trudged up to them. They both turned to the boy, and Charlotte could tell at a glance that he was shaking.

"Max, let's get you into some warm clothes, okay? I'll get you a Sprite when we get in the car, get your blood sugar up a little," Charlotte directed.

She looked over at Noah, seeing the same apprehension she felt mirrored on his face. They worked in perfect unison to get

Max dry and comfortable before they started the long drive back to the hospital.

TWENTY

The perfect, happy bubble of their "day off" popped as soon as they hit the St. Louis city limits. Charlotte was in the back seat of the car with Max, letting him recline in her lap. Max drifted off, exhausted from the day's exertion, and Charlotte did her best to make him comfortable. She kept catching Noah's concerned gaze in the rear view mirror, but he didn't talk much on the drive back.

"I'm going to tell them that Max showed up at my house," Charlotte said. Noah turned to look at her for a brief moment before refocusing on the road.

"Okay," was his only response.

"I'm going to say that I called you to help me convince him to go back to the hospital. Just let me do the talking, or we could both get in a lot of trouble. I'll take him in alone."

Noah looked as if he were about to argue, but then he just nodded. Charlotte looked down at Max, thinking to wake him a few minutes before they reached the hospital. She stilled, realizing that his breath seemed very shallow. She gave him a gentle shake.

"Max?" she asked. No response. "Max? Can you wake up, buddy?"

He opened his eyes and gave her a sleepy smile.

"I'm thirsty," he whispered, his voice thin as a reed.

NOAH'S REVELATION

Charlotte grabbed a bottle of water and handed it to him.

"How are you feeling?" she asked, trying not to seem overly worried.

"Not so good," Max said with a shrug. "I'm glad we went, though. I haven't shifted in weeks."

Charlotte hesitated.

"Listen, Max… About today…"

"I can't tell them that you and Noah took me, right?" Max asked.

"Yeah," Charlotte said, nodding. "I think it would be considered kidnapping, even though you wanted to go."

"Adults are dumb," Max told her, all seriousness.

Charlotte looked up at Noah, finding in his expression the exact same sad humor she felt.

"You're right. But here's the hospital now, so let's you and me get out of the car and I'll take you upstairs, okay?"

"What about Noah?" Max asked.

"Noah will come up in a little while, after I get you settled in," Charlotte promised.

"Will you, Noah?" Max asked.

"You bet. I wouldn't miss it," Noah said.

Charlotte gave him a brief smile before opening the car door and climbing out, then getting Max out. She gave Noah one last look over her shoulder as she settled Max into a wheelchair. He gave her a solemn wave, looking uncertain.

Charlotte straightened her spine and pushed Max toward the elevators.

"Let's go see what kind of trouble we're in, hmm?" she asked Max as they headed upstairs.

TWENTY ONE

"You've got a visitor," Connie called as she stepped into Max's room.

Charlotte pushed upright from her slumped position in the chair next to Max's bed. She cleared her throat and laid the manila folder with Max's latest lab results aside.

"He's still asleep, I'm afraid," Charlotte told Connie.

"For you, not for Max. Or for both, whatever," Connie said, waving a hand. She moved back and Noah appeared in the doorway, filling it with his size and bulk.

"Hey, you," Charlotte said, keeping her words quiet. Noah's gaze flickered from her to Max and back again, a question. Charlotte stood and made her way over to Noah, drawn to him like a magnet. She held out a hand, seeking comfort, and nearly sighed aloud when he took it.

"Let's go get a soda," she suggested, nodding her head at Max. She wanted to talk to Noah about her patient, but not in hearing range.

"Sure. I'm buying," Noah said. His tone was light, clashing with the darkness in his eyes, and Charlotte gave his hand a gentle squeeze.

They headed over to the vending machines in the deserted family lounge, grabbing a couple of sodas before sitting down in the uncomfortable hospital chairs.

"What's the news?" Noah asked. "What happened when you guys got back?"

"Connie was running the floor, and she didn't ask any questions. Just announced that he was back. Dr. Rivers didn't seem too happy, but he wasn't about to lecture Max about it. Not after…" Charlotte paused for a second, taking a sip of her soda as she tried to figure out what to say. "Max is a lot more sick than I realized. His labs from yesterday came back while we were gone and… it doesn't look very good. His white blood cells are almost completely depleted. They may have to move him into an isolation room tonight."

"That's why he's so tired, I guess," Noah said.

Charlotte nodded.

"Yeah. Poor kid," she sighed.

"Did we… did we do him more harm than good by taking him out today? I mean, he ate all that junk food and swam in a river…" Noah's shoulders slumped.

"Honestly, Noah, I don't know. But you can't keep a shifter away from nature for this long. If we hadn't taken him, Max would have run off on his own sooner or later. At least this way he got to have a day of fun and then got back to the hospital in one piece."

"So… what happens now?"

"We wait. If his immune system recovers, he might turn the corner and start recovering. If it doesn't, he'll keep getting worse and worse."

Charlotte felt an odd detachment as she explained it, as if her nurse side was taking over, telling a grieving relative a diagnosis. Inside, she felt all ripped up, sad beyond compare, but years of medical training kept her composed and cool outside.

Noah, on the other hand, looked miserable. He rubbed a massive hand over his face and through his hair, blowing out an angry breath. He braced his elbows on his knees, hanging his head low.

"This is fucking terrible. How do you do this every day?" he asked. His tone was so harsh that Charlotte nearly drew back, but her experience with people's reactions to dire illnesses told her that Noah wasn't upset with her.

"Someone has to do it. Otherwise kids like Max would be all alone," she explained.

Noah looked up at her then, a thousand unnamed emotions swirling in the azure depths of his eyes. Something stirred deep within Charlotte, a wanting. Lust, yes, but something more, too. Something deeper, darker.

"Do you have a ritual for this part, too?" Noah asked.

Charlotte gave him a soft smile and shook her head.

"Usually I drink some good red wine and go to sleep. But tonight… I'd rather just be with you," she told him.

"I can't think of anything I'd like more," Noah told her, standing and drawing Charlotte to her feet.

After stopping to talk to Connie, asking for a phone call if Max's condition worsened even slightly, Charlotte turned the tables and led Noah to the elevators and out of the hospital.

TWENTY TWO

The cab ride and the hotel lobby were fleeting moments for Charlotte; all she could focus on was the press of her body against Noah's in the car, the soft callouses on his palms brushing the bare skin of her arms and wrists. She couldn't think of the elevator ride when Noah dropped burning kisses along her jaw, couldn't see the long hallways when he pulled her against the length of his body to feel his hardness, couldn't think of getting the door open when his nose brushed her ear as he took a long pull of her scent.

When the hotel room door swung shut behind them with a slam, Charlotte turned in Noah's embrace. Sliding her arms around his shoulders, she reached up on her tiptoes and sought his lips, making her desire as blatant as his. Noah pinned her to the wall, knocking a painting to the floor in his fervor. His hands cupped her ass, lifting and sliding her upward as he pressed into her, supporting her as is she were weightless.

One of Noah's hands brushed her shoulder and the nape of her neck before his fingers plunged into her hair, pulling her head back, angling her lips to his pleasure as he plundered her mouth. His kiss was desperate and consuming, deep thrusts of his tongue as he ground his hips against hers.

Charlotte groaned into his mouth, arching her back to move her breasts closer to Noah's enticing heat. She let out a surprised yip when he picked her up and carried her into the hotel's lavish bathroom, setting her on the marble counter.

Noah turned to the huge tiled shower, enclosed only by two thin pieces of glass, and pressed several buttons on the wall. Steaming water burst forth from several shower heads, and fog began to build in the room instantly.

When Noah turned back to her, the intensity in his expression made Charlotte's knees weak. She reached for him, eliciting a growl that reverberated throughout the bathroom. Noah made quick work of stripping himself, no seductive dance or teasing. Still, Charlotte felt her pulse quicken and her eyes go wide as she took in every inch of his tanned, muscular body, hard and ready and hungry for her. She bit her lip as her eyes dipped down to the hard, thick length of his cock.

She startled when Noah closed the space between them, grabbing the hem of her dress and yanking it upward, pulling it off in two jerky motions. He removed her bra and panties the same way, his touch so rough that he actually tore her skimpy black boy shorts.

Charlotte couldn't move, caught under his spell. She stared up at him as he flung her clothes to the side, completely absorbed by the dark, fierce hunger that radiated from Noah's gaze, threatening to burn them both alive. Charlotte shivered, realizing that a part of her wanted that very, very badly.

When Noah grabbed her hips and picked her up again, pressing his cock against the softness of her belly as he carried her into the shower, Charlotte realized how wet she was for him. He stood her in the middle of the shower, just where three separate jets of water met, and stared down at her for several long, trembling seconds.

"What have you done to me?" Noah asked, his voice little more than a rumble in his chest. His eyes searched her face, examined her bare breasts, but he seemed to be speaking more to himself than to her.

"Noah—" Charlotte began, but then he was kissing her again, his lips parting hers, his tongue delving to meet her own in a sweet, hard rhythm that was uniquely Noah's. Hot water spilled over them both, making every tiny contact infinitely more pleasurable.

One of his big hands splayed over her back, bracing her waist, as the other cupped and fondled her breast. The moment that she relaxed under his kiss, he ripped his mouth from hers and used the tip of his tongue to tease and explore her ear, nipping her earlobe with his teeth. Charlotte cried out and squirmed, the sensation sending liquid heat to her nipples and straight down to her core.

She slid one arm around his neck and lifted one knee, rubbing her foot along the hard lines of his ankle and calf. Every inch of him was pure, lean muscle, and damn if it wasn't killing her. She ran her free hand over the ridges of his ribs and hip, sighing with want.

Noah stiffened under her touch, his cock twitching against her stomach giving away his weakness. Charlotte grinned up at him, taking a half step back and running her fingertips down the rippling muscle of his abs, licking her lips as his eyes visibly darkened with carnal lust. When she closed her fingers around his throbbing erection, her big Alpha male actually shivered.

One glide of her hand over his water-slicked cock, one swipe of her thumb over the blunt crown, and she had him right where she wanted him, every muscle bulging as he struggled to remain still and silent, clinging tightly to his last reserve of control.

Heedless of the water coming down around her, Charlotte locked her gaze to Noah's and sank to her knees. His expression turned hard, almost hostile, but he didn't move a muscle. Charlotte deliberately licked her lips again as she stared him down, a direct challenge.

His growl of dominance was cut short when her lips brushed the tip of his cock, parting to let her tongue brush the hot, slick underside of the crown. Noah's hips jerked as he sucked in a huge breath, his growl returning. Instead of stopping her, though, one hand threaded into the damp tumble of her hair, holding her in place.

Charlotte continued to stare right up at Noah as she opened her mouth fully and took him in, as deep as she could manage.

He was too long and thick for her to take him all at once, but she curled her fist around the base of his cock and bobbed her head slowly, enjoying the torment in Noah's eyes.

His fingers tightened in her hair as she worked her tongue around the tip with every movement. She gripped his hip with one hand, keeping him from thrusting into her throat even though she knew he could barely keep himself in check. Instead she kept her rhythm steady, sucking and licking until Noah gave a pained growl.

"Charlotte," Noah hissed, trying to pull her away.

She ignored him, trailing her free hand down between his legs to cup and tease his balls.

"Charlotte," he said again, his voice desperate, nearly threatening.

Noah's whole body vibrated, straining, for several long moments until he stiffened and shouted, his cock pulsing as he came, thrusting hard into her mouth. The salty tang of his seed filled her senses as she licked and sucked him, pushing him through his climax.

Charlotte gasped when Noah's hands pulled her away, lifting her to her feet. If she'd expected him to be replete and relaxed, she couldn't have been more wrong. His mouth came down on hers, as hard and demanding as ever. He backed her into the wall, lifting her off her feet and pinning her into place with his hips.

His lips left hers as he released a tortured groan, one hand cupping her ass as the other explored her breast. She was shocked to feel his cock hardening against her belly once more as he thrust and ground against her soft flesh. Charlotte looked up at him, enthralled by his glowering expression of hungry determination.

He slipped his hand between them, fingers finding and caressing her clit, stoking the flames of her desire. She could still taste him on her lips as his fingers slid down to touch her core, one thick finger sliding deep inside. She cried out and raked her nails over his shoulders, wanting more.

Noah grasped his cock and thrust inside her, stretching and

filling her without hesitation. This time there was no gentle easing, no preparation as he thrust hard into her slick passage, stealing her breath and thoughts as he moved within her.

Noah's hands found her hips, holding her up against the shower wall as he hammered into her, shuddering and panting. The cool tile against her back, the hot water pouring off Noah onto her breasts, the sensation of her nipples against his chest, the look of complete concentration on his face... Charlotte was a living flame, her lips and teeth exploring his neck and shoulder as he fucked her, his cock touching every sensitive spot inside her body. He claimed her, branded her, took and gave everything she'd ever known.

"Noah!" she cried, her body tensing, inner muscles fluttering. She climaxed without warning, pulling them both under, his cry mixing with her own in the steamy air. For several moments, she knew nothing, only the hot, liquid pull of pleasure at her breasts and core and lips.

When she finally sagged against Noah, he let her legs down, both of them standing unsteadily under the now-cooling shower spray. They leaned against each other, struggling for breath, until Charlotte shivered. Then Noah was pulling her out of the shower, pulling her close and picking her up. He wrapped her in a thick, soft towel and carried her to the bed. Setting her down, he vanished for a moment before returning wrapped in his own towel, holding another to spread under her pillow.

Noah pulled back the comforter and climbed underneath and Charlotte followed him, meek as a lamb. He wrapped her in his arms with a sigh, settling her at his side. It was only moments before Charlotte tumbled into a long, dreamless sleep.

TWENTY THREE

When Noah woke, Charlotte was sitting in the chair near the window, staring at her phone with a bleak expression. She wore one of his dress shirts, with only one button done just below her breasts, and Noah immediately wanted her again, his body hardening. The look on her face kept him from pouncing on her, though.

"Is there news?" he asked, rising and stretching. Charlotte took in his nudity with a raised brow and a bemused smile, shaking her head.

"Nothing yet. I'm going a little crazy," she admitted.

Noah grabbed a fresh pair of boxer briefs and a t-shirt from his suitcase and tugged them on before taking the chair across from hers. He pushed his briefcase over on the table and leaned across the table, taking her hand.

"I can't believe you do this with all your patients. It would kill a normal person," Noah told her.

She blushed and shook her head again.

"I don't. I mean, I care for every patient. But Max is special to me."

"I can see why. He's an incredible kid, really smart. He's got a good heart under all the hurt and anger from being in the foster system. I can't believe his people haven't taken him in," Noah grumbled.

Charlotte's chest rose as she sucked in a deep breath. She turned that dazzling sapphire gaze on Noah, nearly stilling his heartbeat.

"I've filled out the paperwork to become an adoptive parent. I'm just too much of a coward to file it," she said.

Noah's jaw actually dropped. Of all the things he could have expected her to say, this certainly wasn't among them.

"You… you want to adopt Max?" he asked, trying to keep his voice level. He let the idea sink in, picturing Max in Charlotte's front yard, imagining the two of them arm-in-arm. It was sweet, but…

"I filled the papers out the last time he was in the hospital. I did a lot of research, and…"

Charlotte shrugged, pulling her hand away and looking down into her lap.

"Why haven't you done it?"

She looked up, surprised.

"It's a big responsibility," she said. "I'd have to sell my house, get a bigger place, closer to a good school district. And I work a lot, so that would be really hard."

Before Noah could say anything else, Charlotte gave herself a hard shake.

"Can we not talk about this anymore? It feels a little morbid."

Noah looked her over, sighing internally at her discomfort.

"I want to show you something," he said. He opened his briefcase and pulled out his laptop, pulling up his most recent photo set. He turned the laptop toward Charlotte, smiling at the way her eyes widened.

"You took these?" she asked, scrolling through dozens of photos of Max.

"I did."

"These are amazing. You can't even tell that he's sick!" she said.

"I asked him if I could interview him, and his stipulation was that he look healthy in the photos. I touched them up a little," Noah admitted.

Charlotte looked up at him, biting her lip. She hesitated, then sucked in a breath.

"Can I read your interview?" she asked, her voice barely above a whisper.

"Sure," Noah said. He pulled up the document and then stood. "I'm heading for the shower. Make yourself at home."

Noah dragged himself to the shower, growing irritated as his seeming inability to leave Charlotte alone for a handful of minutes. She was probably sick of him by now. So he went through the motions of taking a shower, scrubbing and washing, trying not to sigh like a lovesick schoolboy. The thought made him pause, scowl, and then bang his head against the cool tile wall. *Love* was not in Noah's vocabulary.

"I am so fucked," he said aloud. "So, so fucked if I'm even thinking about that word."

He turned off the shower and dried off, wrapping a towel around his waist. The second that he stepped out of the bathroom, Charlotte almost gave him a heart attack. She flung herself into his arms, giving him a long, desperate kiss. When she wrapped her arms and legs around Noah and dragged him down to the bed, there wasn't an ounce of resistance in him. Frustration over a certain four-letter word fled, banished by Charlotte's unmistakable and considerable charms.

TWENTY FOUR

"My brain feels like it's full of mush," Charlotte groused, turning over and pressing her sweat-slicked naked body against his.

"Really? I felt that way two orgasms ago," Noah informed her.

Charlotte giggled, pressing her lips to his. He'd never seen her so lighthearted, and it made him feel good. Better than he had since he'd touched down on American soil, in fact. Still, he supposed that they should do something other than fuck. Charlotte had seemed a little sore at the beginning of the last round, and if they didn't get out of bed soon he was going to have her again anyway. Minx that she was, she would probably let him.

"Okay. What's on the menu today. Are you working?" he asked.

"No," Charlotte snorted. "Now's a nice time to ask, since it's probably noon. Anyway, I think I should go check on Max. After yesterday…"

"We should go, you mean," Noah said, giving her a look.

Her tentative smile made his stomach do uncomfortable things.

"All right," she agreed.

"I'm afraid that means you'll have to put on clothes," he told her with a frown.

Charlotte laughed and rolled her eyes, giving him a tantalizing view as she climbed out of bed and found her clothes. Where she led, Noah could only but follow, so he got up and got dressed too.

Driving to Children's Hospital, Noah was filled with nervous energy. He couldn't get the image of Charlotte and Max hugging out of his mind, like it was burned into the back of his brain. He felt as though he was at the edge of something, but damn if he wanted to explore any further. He'd quit his traveling job, he'd found a girl that he might just be serious about... he was already outside his comfort zone. Way outside of it, in fact.

"What?" Charlotte asked, giving him a skeptical look.

"What?" he asked.

"You keep heaving these big sighs. Care to share?"

Noah arched a brow, pursing his lips.

"Definitely not," he said. "And look, we're already here."

He pulled into a space in the parking lot, jumping out to open Charlotte's door. She gave him a knowing look, but didn't press the issue. Noah took Charlotte's hand and they headed upstairs, the path already familiar to him.

"Nurses' station is empty," Charlotte noted with a frown.

They passed it and stopped in front of Max's room. Finding the door closed, Noah reached out and knocked. No response. Noah swung the door wide, freezing in place when he found it perfectly empty.

"Max?" he called out, feeling stupid even as the word left his mouth.

Noah stepped into the room, Charlotte on his heels, clinging to his arm.

"No," she whispered. "No no no!"

Noah looked down at Charlotte as she crumpled. He caught her as a sob burst from her chest, her eyes going wild as she scanned the room.

"We're too late," she uttered. "He'll never even know..."

"Darling, you don't know—" Noah tried.

"He's *dead*, Noah! We're too late!" Charlotte cried.

She looked up at him, devastated. In that moment, Noah saw the image of her and Max again. This time, though, he was on

Max's other side, all three of them beaming. The idea, the very image Noah had pushed away since their time at the beach, hit him like a fist to the gut. Looking at that same feeling as it spread across Charlotte's face tore at his heart.

He gathered her in his arms, hugging her tightly.

"I'm so sorry, darling," he murmured into her hair. "I'm so sorry. If I hadn't taken him out yesterday…"

"What the hell are you two doing in here?" came a man's voice.

Noah and Charlotte turned to find a short, silver-haired man standing in the door. He wore a long white doctor's coat and held a stack of charts.

"Dr. Rivers," Charlotte said, her voice wavering.

"You're not working," he said. More a statement than a question. He eyed Noah for a moment, then looked around the room. Something seemed to dawn on him, and he cleared his throat.

"Ah. Your young friend Max," he said. "He's been transferred to D ward."

Noah let out a grunt of surprise. Charlotte gripped his harm, her nails digging into his skin.

"Transferred?" she repeated.

"Your friend Connie got him into the new chemotherapy trial that's about to start. I hear they're having remarkable results. I wish I could get more of my patients into it," Dr. Rivers said, cocking his head.

"I thought—" Charlotte spun around and flung herself into Noah's arms once more, sobs wracking her body again.

"I'll leave you to it," the doctor said, giving them a disapproving glance as he went.

"Hey, hey," Noah said, trying to soothe her. "Everything is okay, darling."

Charlotte calmed in his embrace, taking in a ragged breath.

"The papers," she said, turning her tear-streaked face up to him.

"Papers?" he asked, brushing a lock of hair back from her face.

"I need to file the adoption papers," she said, her brow creasing.

Noah hesitated for the briefest moment before shaking his head.

"I think you should wait a few days," he said.

Charlotte's eyes widening, anger brewing. She put a hand on his chest, about to push him away, but he trapped her hand and held her there.

"I think we should file some other papers first," he said.

Charlotte's jaw dropped. She looked at him as if he'd gone mad.

"Are you... what?" she asked, confused.

"Charlotte, I want you to be my mate."

Her mouth opened and closed several times as she sputtered.

"You're just... you don't mean that!" she accused.

"I mean every word of it. You are beautiful and fiery and loving, and you somehow manage to tolerate me. I can't think of a woman better suited to me. Can you?" Noah asked, unable to resist teasing her a little.

"What about Max?" she asked, her big blue eyes filling with tears again.

"Well, that's why you should wait. Just until we get human marriage papers, I mean. We should make it official, shouldn't we?"

For a heart-wrenchingly long series of seconds, Noah wasn't certain if she would accept or punch him in the face. Her lips trembled, a single tear spilling down her cheek. He held her hand to his chest, directly over his heart, and held his breath. More than that; for the first time in his life, Noah Beran actually *prayed* for Charlotte to accept his proposal.

"Yes," Charlotte whispered at last.

"Yes?" Noah asked, a grin lighting up his face. The terrible feeling in the pit of his stomach vanished as he watched a hopeful smile light Charlotte's eyes.

"Yes, yes," Charlotte laughed, wiping at her face.

Noah wrapped his arms around her and picked her up,

kissing her for all he was worth. When he set her back on her feet, they were both breathless.

"First things first," he told her. "We visit Max, and then…" He looked at his watch. "We can still make it to the courthouse this afternoon. You won't mind terribly if we sign the papers before you pick out a ring, will you?"

Charlotte gave a watery laugh and shook her head.

"As long as you keep giving me those kisses, I think I might let it slide."

Noah couldn't do anything else but oblige the woman who was destined to be his one true mate.

WANT MORE?

Not so fast! These white-hot Alpha bears have only just begun to thrill you. Noah's Revelation, the second full-length book in the Red Lodge Bears series, available now on Amazon! **Turn to the next page for a glimpse of Gavin and Faith's story.**

GAVIN'S SALVATION

"Come here," Gavin told Faith. "Let me hold you."

He pulled her close, turning so that her back rested against the pool's edge. He kissed her deeply, sweeping his hands up from her waist to her ribs, waiting until her breathing grew heavy once more before bringing his hands up to cup the fullness of her breasts.

Faith responded instantly, giving a soft moan as she arched into his touch.

"I like that sound you make, Faith," he encouraged her. "It's so sexy. Moan for me, Faith."

He brushed his thumbs over her nipples, moving closer until his erection pressed into her belly. She gave another little moan, her eyes drifting closed, her tongue darting out to wet her lips. He brushed his lips over her neck, her collarbone, working her up to more.

Gavin took her mouth, nipping her bottom lip, enjoying the pleasured yip that escaped her. He lifted her by the waist, settling her on the pool's ledge. Before she could squirm or decry her nudity, Gavin lifted one supple breast, placing hot kisses just outside the rosy ring of her nipple.

"Oh!" she cried, her fingernails raking his shoulders.

His very male chuckle was almost more than she could stand.

ALSO BY KAYLA GABRIEL

Alpha Guardians
See No Evil
Hear No Evil
Speak No Evil
Bear Risen
Bear Razed
Bear Reign

GET A FREE BOOK!

Join my mailing list to be the first to know of new releases, free books, special prices and other author giveaways.

http://freeshifterromance.com

ABOUT THE AUTHOR

Kayla Gabriel lives in the wilds of Minnesota where she swears she sees shifters in the woods beyond her yard. Her favorite things in life are mini marshmallows, coffee and when people use their blinker.

Connect with Kayla by
email: kaylagabrielauthor@gmail.com and be sure to get her
FREE book: freeshifterromance.com

http://kaylagabriel.com

www.ingramcontent.com/pod-product-compliance
Lightning Source LLC
LaVergne TN
LVHW011846060526
838200LV00054B/4191